The Melting of
Maggie Bean

The Melting of Maggie Bean

TRICIA RAYBURN

m!x

ALADDIN MIX

NEW YORK   LONDON   TORONTO   SYDNEY

This book is a work of fiction. Any references to historical events, real people, or real locales are used fictitiously. Other names, characters, places, and incidents are the product of the author's imagination, and any resemblance to actual events or locales or persons, living or dead, is entirely coincidental.

ALADDIN MIX

Simon & Schuster Children's Publishing Division

1230 Avenue of the Americas, New York, NY 10020

Text copyright © 2007 by Tricia Rayburn

All rights reserved, including the right of reproduction in whole or in part in any form.

ALADDIN MIX is a trademark of Simon & Schuster, Inc.

ALADDIN PAPERBACKS and related logo are registered trademarks of Simon & Schuster, Inc.

Designed by Christopher Grassi

The text of this book was set in Garamond.

Manufactured in the United States of America

First Aladdin Mix edition April 2007

10 9 8 7 6 5 4 3 2

Library of Congress Control Number 2006931403

ISBN-13: 978-1-4169-3348-9

ISBN-10: 1-4169-3348-4

For Mom, my biggest fan—good things are coming!
And for Michael, who is the very best of everything good.

The Melting of Maggie Bean grew from a graduate writing assignment into an actual book because of the amazing support and enthusiasm of many people. I'd like to thank Lou Ann Walker, my thesis advisor, who first encouraged me to venture into the real (scary!) world of publishing. Infinite "warm fuzzies" go to Rebecca Sherman, my brilliant agent, and Jen Klonsky, my incredible editor, who have made getting picked last in gym class *so* worth it. I am forever grateful to Mom, Kristin, Sean, and Honey, for their willingness to celebrate every new written word, and for being the best family ever. And my endless love and gratitude go to Michael, who makes my biggest dreams a very wonderful reality, every single day.

1. Maggie Bean stood at the chocolate end of the candy aisle, biting her lip and carefully deciding which bag was going to help her survive the next seven days. Gummi Bears, Twizzlers, and Skittles had less fat than Butterfinger, Milky Way, and Nestlé Crunch, and would therefore be the better, healthier options, but "Wild Cherry" and "Banana Berry" never melted in her mouth the way smooth, old-fashioned milk chocolate did. It was the same tough decision every week, because Maggie never considered the best, healthiest option: leaving the store without any candy at all.

" 'Scuse me, miss," a sales clerk said, sounding slightly annoyed.

He stood just behind her, waiting to wheel a cart of vitamins to the pharmacy counter. She apologized quickly, stepped aside, and looked down, her face turning red. Her face was always turning red these days, in gym class or walking uphill from the bus stop, but also in less strenuous situations, like when a teacher called on her unexpectedly or she got the best grade on a French test. Classmates had taken to asking if she was okay, and while she knew she should be thankful for their concern, she only felt worse when the red deepened to maroon at the unwanted attention.

"You know, we just got in a new shipment of Snack-Well's cookies," the sales clerk whispered as he rolled the cart past her. "Chocolate chip, only one hundred twenty calories and four point five grams of fat per serving!" He nodded and smiled. She recognized him from previous weeks, and while she wasn't surprised he remembered her, she was still embarrassed he knew her shopping habits.

When the sales clerk finally reached the end of the aisle and rounded the corner, out of sight, she picked up a bag of Peanut M&M's and another bag of miniature Snickers. Single servings never lasted long enough. These were big bags, like those her mother brought home for trick-or-treaters on Halloween. They were $2.99 each, and she was debating whether she had enough money for both bags *and* a pack of watermelon Bubble Yum when she heard familiar giggles floating from a few aisles down.

Maggie hugged the plastic bags to her chest and tiptoed down the candy aisle. The drugstore sales clerk was the only person who knew how she spent her weekly allowance, and she wanted to keep it that way. When she reached the boxes of Dots and Good & Plenty (which she barely ever glanced at en route to the chocolate), she held her breath and listened.

Anabel Richards and Julia Swanson, Water Wings cocaptains. She'd spent so much time trying to drown out their high-pitched laughter in school that she recognized it immediately. Running into *anyone* from school would've been completely mortifying, but it was just her luck that the captains of the synchronized swim team had chosen *this* day and *this* drugstore to go beauty supply shopping.

Maggie closed her eyes, hurried back down the aisle, and tried not to panic. Every girl in the seventh grade, Maggie included, had spent her childhood hoping to one day be a member of the prestigious team, practicing graceful turns in the bathtub and, later, more sophisticated moves in the town pool. Maggie's desire had always been especially strong, because when her mother was in junior high, she'd been a founding Water Wings team member. If her mother had glory days like former high school star quarterbacks did, those were hers. A Rubbermaid bin filled with ribbons, trophies, and photo albums sat in the attic as proof.

Though she never pressured Maggie to follow in her footsteps, her mother used to joke that Maggie learned the team's signature moves before she learned to walk. She didn't joke anymore. Today's team was superexclusive, and not only did each member have to know how to raise her limbs in and out of pool water with ease, she also had to look appropriate in the silver two-piece that served as the team uniform.

Maggie peered over the plastic bags at her belly. The summer before, she'd been thrilled to find a plain black one-piece swimsuit with an attached waist ruffle. So thrilled, in fact, that she almost hadn't cared when a pregnant woman and a grandmother each bought the same exact one right before she did. She wouldn't have even noticed *that* if the cashier hadn't given her (and her belly) a weird look before ringing her up.

She tiptoed quickly back to the chocolate section. She had three possible options: calmly leave the store without candy and ruin her entire week, calmly leave the store *with* candy and pretend like she could care less if anyone spotted her with ten thousand unnecessary calories in her hands, or book it as fast as possible before the school's biggest glamour girls looked up from their lip gloss.

Maggie raised the bags of candy to her face and inhaled deeply before gently placing them on the shelf. She trailed her fingers over the reassuring Snickers logo, poked fondly at the bright wrappings, and, head down, calmly walked down the aisle, back toward the boxes of Dots and Good & Plenty and the store's exit.

As the sweet chocolate scent faded behind her, Maggie paused, glanced quickly toward the makeup aisle, and spun around. She raced back to the chocolate section and grabbed the two bags she'd just put down plus a bag of miniature Twix.

Avoiding seven whole days without chocolate was worth seven seconds of embarrassment.

She clutched the bags to her chest, dashed down the aisle toward the cash register, and unloaded that week's survival kit on the counter. Her heart pounded and her palms grew damp as she fumbled through her green plastic change purse and the giggles grew louder. She turned her head to see Anabel and Julia whispering and walking toward the counter, carrying pink mascara wands and lipstick tubes. Desperate, Maggie threw all of her loose dollars and coins down without counting, grabbed the candy without waiting for a plastic bag, and ran through the drugstore door.

In her mother's rusty Toyota Camry, Maggie shoved the

M&M's, Snickers, and Twix into her backpack. Her mother usually took forty-five minutes to shop. Maggie usually spent twenty of those minutes in the drugstore making her selection, and the other twenty-five relaxing in the car and dipping into her purchases. Anabel and Julia's mascara search barely left her enough time to hide the evidence.

Leaning across the driver's seat, Maggie scanned the checkout line through the grocery store windows. Relieved to find the coast still clear, she slid down the ripped vinyl seat, caught her breath, and reached for the Twix.

2. "Okay, girls, you know the drill! Four times around the track makes a mile!" Ms. Pinkerton called to the group stretching on the pavement.

"But I have *cramps*, Ms. Pinkerton," Genevieve Snodgrass whined, clutching her stomach and looking pained.

"And I have hemorrhoids. Who cares?" Ms. Pinkerton said without looking up from her clipboard.

Maggie raised her eyebrows and shook her head at her best friend, Aimee McDougall, who reached for her toes nearby. Ms. Pinkerton was new this year. When the girls had first spotted her across the gym in September, they'd assumed she was the guys' coach. She was tall and stocky with short blond hair always hidden underneath a Yankees baseball hat. She wore long T-shirts over long shorts and barked orders in gym class the same way the guys' football coach barked orders on the field.

"Okay!" Ms. Pinkerton clapped her hands together. "Let's line up, front and center, along that yellow line!"

"I hate this," Maggie whispered.

"Beats Madame DuMonde's pop quizzes." Aimee shuddered.

"French can be tough," Maggie agreed. "But I'd give up English forever if it meant never having to run another mile."

Ms. Pinkerton slowly raised the dreaded stopwatch in the air.

"Ms. Pinkerton?" Maggie called.

"What? Who's that? Who said my name?" Ms. Pinkerton eyed the girls from above her oversize purple sunglasses.

"Is it okay if we have to walk at some point?" Maggie timidly waved her hand.

"Walk? Did you say *walk*, Ms. Bean? Am I hearing you correctly?"

"Yes. I just mean, you know, after running for a while, if we have to catch our breath or something?"

Ms. Pinkerton walked toward Maggie.

"Ms. Bean, you *are* familiar with the President's Challenge?"

Maggie nodded.

"The national President's Challenge, the same fitness

program in which you participated just one year ago?" Ms. Pinkerton quickly took off her sunglasses and made Maggie meet her eyes.

"Yes, of course." Though she'd never heard of the President's Challenge before the first week of sixth grade, it had been too torturous to ever forget.

"Then you're familiar with the one-mile *run*, are you not? Do you really think a one-mile *walk* would be appropriate for the demanding, yet fair, President's Challenge?"

Maggie saw beads of sweat pop up along Ms. Pinkerton's forehead and chin. She shook her head.

"So we're clear, then?"

Maggie nodded, her face turning red. She hated the president for making her do this. She bet his officials never said, "Okay, Mr. President, it's that time of year again! Put that bill aside! Situps and pushups, sixty seconds, GO!" And even if his officials *did* say that, at least the president didn't have to sweat in front a big group of other presidents.

"You okay?" Aimee whispered. She stood beside Maggie and put one hand on her shoulder as Ms. Pinkerton resumed her position on the side of the track and reraised the stopwatch.

Maggie shrugged and looked down at her sneakers. There was no denying the embarrassment, because Aimee knew her too well. They'd been best friends since the fourth grade, when Maggie's self-confidence was still intact and she hadn't thought twice about inviting over the most popular girl in her class.

"Okay, ladies! On your marks!"

Maggie stepped one foot back, leaned forward, and rested her fingertips on the track. She focused on the toe of her sneaker instead of the jumbo marshmallow her right calf had become.

"Get set!"

She raised her head, trying not to notice the defined calf of the girl in front of her, the sharp edge of muscle that looked like it could poke out Maggie's eye if she shifted in the wrong direction. Her heart raced and she reassured herself that gym class only lasted forty-five minutes, and they needed at least ten minutes to change before next period, so the agony couldn't last that much longer.

"GO!" Ms. Pinkerton yelled, and blew her whistle.

As the group shuffled away from the yellow line, Maggie tried to console herself with the idea that she should feel sorry for Ms. Pinkerton for being so insecure and unhappy that she needed to control kids with a whistle to feel better.

"Doing okay, Mags?" Aimee asked after the first half of the first lap.

"Great!" Maggie gulped. "I've got at least three minutes before my lungs pop."

"Just remember, two counts in, two counts out. In through your nose, out through your mouth."

"No offense, Aim"—Maggie swallowed—"but I'm just going to hold my breath till the finish line." She spoke without inhaling, her words bouncing with every step.

"You'll pass out long before then." Aimee's words, on the other hand, flowed from her mouth as though she stood completely still. "Just pace yourself. Don't try to overdo it. And don't think too much."

Maggie laughed. "Right." Her breathing issues, the aching in her shins, tightness in her calves, and pain in her side made it impossible to do anything *but* think—about how her body was going to break apart.

"McDougall!" Ms. Pinkerton shouted.

Aimee spun around and raised one hand against the glare of the sun.

"You're already two minutes behind last semester's time!"

"So?" Aimee shouted, jogging backward.

"So you're an athlete, not a cheerleader! Get moving!"

Maggie almost tripped when Anabel Richards came up beside them, already into her second lap. "Ms. P said she'll give the first five across the finish line extra credit."

Maggie's mouth, already wide for maximum air intake, fell open even farther as two more Water Wings joined them. Gym was the one class in which she could actually *use* the extra credit, and she certainly needed it more than anyone who could make it to the finish line without an oxygen tank.

"Thanks," Aimee said, "but—"

"Aim," Maggie interjected, brushing strands of damp hair from her cheeks and tugging at the back of her T-shirt, "just *go*." She playfully nudged her toward the Water Wings. She knew Aimee could've been around the track three times already if not for her.

"Okay," Aimee relented, "but I *will* meet you at the finish line."

As her best friend dashed away with the Water Wings, their laughter fading as the distance increased, Maggie tried to ignore the ponytails bouncing ahead of her. She tried to ignore the elastic waistband of her shorts that dug into her waist, the mesh material that kept rising up her inner thighs as they rubbed together, and the subtle kicks she performed to give the shorts room to fall back in place. She felt her butt and stomach jiggle with each step, and she thought of her French assignment, the 98 percent she'd gotten on the math exam (the only A in the class), the 100 percent she'd received on her earth science presentation, and the smile she thought Peter Applewood had given her at their lockers earlier.

She would think about these things because she had to keep her feet moving. No matter what, no matter the pain in her side, the tightness in her calves, or the ponytails bobbing around her, she would keep her feet moving.

Walking was *not* an option.

3. It was just her luck that of all the combinations of all the lockers in the entire school, Maggie was stuck with 36-24-36. She'd seen enough *Cosmo* and *Glamour* covers to know that her forty-two-inch chest, thirty-four-inch waist and fourty-four-inch hips were better suited to a polar bear, and now she'd be reminded every weekday between September and June for the next two years. There was only one way to deal, besides carrying nine textbooks, four notebooks, and her jacket with her all day, and that was to pretend the combination numbers were associated with something else.

(Because she *had* to deal. Her future relationship with Peter Applewood depended on their chance locker encounters!)

Thirty-six phone calls, twenty-four dates, thirty-six kisses.

She spun the dial and opened the locker door. She needed chances, but she didn't need one right then, when her face still radiated more heat than the sun and her thick, dark hair clung to the back of her neck in sticky clumps. She'd crossed the yellow line for the fourth time in just under eighteen minutes, which was almost six over the suggested President's Challenge maximum, and had had a hard time accomplishing even that. The other girls had already begun the journey across the soccer field toward the gym, and Maggie had been so far behind that Aimee had closed her eyes while sitting on the bleachers waiting for her and hadn't seen her final approach. She'd finished hot and tired, but happy, because she'd shuffled, scuffed, even skipped in some places, but she hadn't walked.

She threw her math book onto the top shelf and reached for her French book. As she rummaged through papers, she thought about how happy she was not having a small mirror hanging in her locker. She was probably the only girl in her class without one, but why would she ever want to be reminded of her shapeless brown hair, boring brown eyes, and puffy cheeks? Especially now, when she really needed to find her book and didn't have time to feel bad about her reflection.

Where *was* her French book? She hadn't taken it home

the night before because they'd watched French cartoons in class while Madame DuMonde read *People* magazine, and been given a night free of homework so long as they promised not to tell their parents about Madame's afternoon off. Maggie sifted through her other books and notebooks, hurrying to beat the bell.

Her face grew redder, her forehead damper from sticky bangs and a fresh wave of perspiration. The voices around her faded as students moved out of the hallway and into classrooms. Maggie unloaded her locker, stacking one book after another onto the floor, not noticing when the stack grew so tall it wobbled briefly before toppling around her feet. She looked in her backpack again, brushed her damp hair away from her face, and closed her eyes to remember exactly where she'd last seen it. She pictured the cover, red with a silver-gray Tour Eiffel and miniature French men and women, wearing berets and sitting at adjacent outdoor cafés, and in the background—

"Maggie?"

Her eyes snapped open and she looked straight ahead.

Peter Applewood stood there, waiting for her to respond.

She quickly picked up a couple of books from the floor

and tossed them back into her locker, trying to hide her face behind the open door.

"Peter, hi! How's it going? Sorry about the mess. I'll be right out of your way."

"Were you looking for something in particular?"

She stood up, brushed her hair back, and straightened her sweatshirt.

"Yes, a book. I have no idea—"

She stopped talking as her eyes registered the bright red cover of the book he held.

"Where did you, I mean, how did you—?"

He raised his eyebrows, smiled, and shrugged. Maggie put one hand on her stomach, trying to reassure it enough so that it would stop turning.

"I didn't realize what it was when I grabbed it out of my locker this morning."

He handed her the book and Maggie opened it. There it was, *Maggie Bean*, on the front page.

She looked up. "It was in *your* locker?" She scrunched her face.

"I guess you threw it in there accidentally."

She smiled weakly. "That sounds like something I would do."

"Need help?" He motioned to the floor.

"What?" She'd already forgotten about the remaining mess surrounding her. "Oh, that." She waved her hand. "No, thanks. It won't take long."

She knew he could hear her heart pounding; it must have been shaking the walls of the school. And even if he didn't and it wasn't, there was no missing the inferno face she was surely sporting. If he stood around her any longer, he might start sweating himself.

"Thank you for this." She patted the book and stuffed it into her backpack without meeting his eyes. She tugged at the back of her sweatshirt as she pretended to look for something else. She wasn't about to bend over and draw attention to her least favorite physical feature for the sake of cleaning.

"No problem." He opened his locker, put a book away, and took one out. "Everything else going okay?"

"Sure, yup, sweet as pie." She closed her eyes and shook her head as soon as the words left her mouth. Leave it to her to include unnecessary baked goods in what could've easily been a normal response.

He laughed. "Great." He closed his locker and smiled. "Well, I'll see you later, then."

She tried to smile and waved. She didn't turn to watch him the way she might've under other, less mortifying circumstances, so she settled for picturing his short, black hair and khaki Nike hat, plaid button-down shirt, and jeans, and his easy walk retreating down the hallway. He was on the baseball team and had the unhurried stroll of an athlete.

And here she stood, anything *but* an athlete, sweaty, red, embarrassed, and wondering how she could convince the administration to move her locker assignment to the other side of the building.

When the bell rang, Maggie threw the rest of her books inside the locker and hurried to class, cutting through the girl's bathroom to get there faster, and covering her face with her red French textbook as she passed in front of the mirrors.

4. "So, how were our days?"
Maggie's mother asked brightly as she unfolded a paper napkin in her lap.

"Fine." Maggie reached for the mashed potatoes. "Are these real or from the box?"

"Dudley's Spuds were on sale this week." Her mother cleared her throat and reached for the glass of water next to her plate.

"Boxed potatoes are cheaper than actual potatoes?" Maggie frowned and handed the bowl to Summer without scooping any onto her plate. Ever since their father lost his job, their mother had taken to attacking the coupon flyer as soon as the Sunday paper hit their yard. For six months each meal had become more boring than the one before.

"This week they are." Her mother speared a drumstick with her fork. "Chicken?"

Her father held out his plate.

"I got a letter from my pen pal in Texas," Summer offered.

Maggie grabbed two rolls and passed around the bread basket. When everyone else took only one, she sheepishly put back the second.

As it was, her waist spilled over the top of her jeans, her chest rested comfortably on a fat roll, and her cotton T-shirt sleeves clung to her arms like spandex. She was already the Pillsbury Doughgirl. There was no need to test the effects of an extra roll.

"I told Aunt Violetta that you're going with her to the next Pound Patrollers meeting." Her father spoke like it was just another after-school activity.

Maggie's mouth fell open as her head snapped up. Two rolls were riskier than she'd thought. *"What?"*

"Pen pal?" Summer suggested weakly. "Texas? Far, far away?"

When his mouth continued to fill with food instead of explanation, Maggie looked to her mom.

"Chicken?" she asked brightly, raising the platter for distraction.

"Next Wednesday," he continued, shoving a forkful of potatoes into his mouth and talking around it. "Seven o'clock."

"You're kidding, right?" Maggie shook her head. "Please tell me you're kidding."

Aunt Violetta, her father's sister, had had weight issues her entire life and really *needed* to attend those meetings. According to him, she'd married the first guy who kissed her because she'd been afraid no one else would ever want to kiss her again, and Maggie just didn't feel they were playing in the same ballpark. She'd heard her aunt's stories, knew the embarrassment involved. The weigh-ins, the oversize doctor's scale, the circle of unhappy, middle-aged women whining about their reasons for eating three too many slices of birthday cake (which, Maggie reasoned, was way different from eating two barely-there dinner rolls).

"Maggie, we know you've put on a bit of weight recently. What is it up to now? Thirty pounds?" He raised his eyebrows, then continued when she slumped in her chair without answering. "We just want you to be healthy." He looked at her pointedly, as though he was doing her the favor she wouldn't do for herself.

"But I can't go!" She bit her lip, surprised at the outburst.

There was no denying her recent weight gain. Just one

month before, the nurse had clucked her tongue so loudly during her annual school physical that Maggie couldn't help but look at the scale. Her mouth had dropped at the 181, which was 32 pounds higher than the year before. But she'd still run one thousand track laps before she'd go to a single Pound Patrollers meeting.

He lowered his fork and looked at her. "And why not?"

She cleared her throat and brushed her hair away from her face. "Wednesdays aren't good for me." She tried to sound casual, as though the reason was anything other than the fact that attending those meetings would be social devastation. "It's a really big homework night. *Huge*, actually." She directed this to her mother, who proudly displayed every report card, certificate, and trophy. "I mean, papers, presentations, tests, pop quizzes. Always on Thursdays." She shrugged as though there was simply nothing she could do.

"Maggie." He tilted his head. "It's for your own good."

"She's from Amarillo!" Summer exclaimed. "Like arma-dillo!"

Maggie's mother patted Summer's hand.

Maggie felt the familiar heat spring to her cheeks. She pushed her plate away and shoved her chair back.

"Where are you going?"

"Mondays are really big homework nights too," she said

quickly, cringing when she heard her voice quiver. It didn't matter that she'd finished her assignments before dinner. It was the only reason she could think of to escape from the table as fast as possible.

"Maggie, honey," her mother gently protested. "Please sit down."

"Dinner was delicious, Mom." She smiled without looking up as she cleared her place.

"But I didn't tell you what my pen pal said!"

Maggie paused, plate in one hand, silverware in the other. She was only ten years old, but Summer had become Maggie's biggest ally over the past six months.

"Sorry, Summer." She frowned. "Later, I promise."

Underneath her comforter and with her headphones on, Maggie unwrapped and swallowed more mini Snickers and Milky Ways than a trick-or-treater could fit into a plastic orange pumpkin. Even her favorite iTunes playlist, "Diva-licious," with Kelly Clarkson, Mariah Carey, Christina Aguilera, Shakira, and the Dixie Chicks, couldn't lift her mood.

Her laptop glowed in front of her, its keyboard blanketed by wrappers. She stared at the Excel spreadsheet as she chewed and swallowed without tasting, clicking on the labeled tabs that lined the bottom of the screen: Daily

Assignments, Weekly Assignments, Upcoming Tests, Grades, Long-Term Academic Goals, After-School Activities. Maintaining straight As was hard work, and she'd started Maggie's Master Multitasker spreadsheet the year before. She updated it every night, ranking assignments in order of importance, checking them off as they were completed, recording every grade as it was received, and outlining future aspirations. It gave her goosebumps to see an entire page of A plusses or column of checkmarks.

But Maggie's Master Multitasker also reminded her of areas needing improvement. And those were noted by the very last tab on the bottom of the spreadsheet.

She reached without looking into the plastic bag next to her, grabbed a handful of M&M's, and clicked on "Miscellaneous."

She sighed around a gob of chocolate as the page loaded. The same two tasks had been listed for months:

#1: Win over Peter Applewood with charm, intellect, and wit.

#2: Lose weight (in case charm, intellect, and wit backfire).

They were the only two items she could never check off. And it drove her crazy.

She swallowed, licked her lips and fingertips, and brushed

off the keyboard. She thought carefully, and then added another, potentially uncheckable item.

#3: DISAPPEAR ON WEDNESDAYS.

She highlighted the new entry, saved the changes, closed the laptop, and pushed it toward the foot of her bed. She grabbed the phone from her nightstand and dialed without having to look at the number pad. The phone rang and rang till the familiar answering machine picked up.

"Aim, I hope your night was better than mine! Give me a call."

Maggie hung up the phone and quickly unwrapped and swallowed two more Twix bars without thinking. She shoved the wrappers and half-empty candy bags off her bed and to the floor and curled on her side.

As the last bit of chocolate slid down her throat, Maggie thought about the mile run and the Peter Applewood locker incident. She thought about not having a date to the prom and not fitting into the black formal wrap all senior girls wear for their senior portraits. She thought about these things, even though they were five years away, because she just assumed the planets and the stars had all gotten together and decided that this was her fate. She would just be this miserable forever, and she might as well enjoy the chocolate and caramel, because that was all she was going to get.

5. "Oh my gosh, did you see?" Aimee's long blond hair flew behind her as she ran to where Maggie sat in the cafeteria.

"Did I see what?" Maggie closed her earth science book and swallowed the last of her pizza.

"The notice!"

"About the chess championships? Even *I'm* managing to keep my cool about that one."

"Right above that one. The purple paper, about Water Wings!"

Maggie rolled her eyes. "Yes, whoop-de-do, two spots have opened for the season. Big deal."

"Not just any spots," Aimee said, dropping her backpack to the floor, resting her lunch tray on the table, and sitting across from Maggie. "Two *seventh-grade* spots." She smiled wide, her blue eyes brighter than the sapphires in Maggie's mom's favorite section of the JCPenney catalog.

Maggie raised her eyebrows and tilted her head, still unsure as to Aimee's obvious excitement. A very limited number of Water Wings slots were allotted to seventh graders, leaving the team primarily comprised of eighth graders, but she still didn't understand why she should care.

Aimee grabbed Maggie's hands across the table and squeezed them. "I think we should try out."

Maggie snorted so hard that her nose burned with the iced tea she'd just sipped. *"We?"* They'd been over this. Maggie was *not* Water Wings material.

"Yes, *we*," Aimee repeated firmly, as though Maggie should know better than to think her friend would do it without her.

"Um, have you looked at me recently?"

"Of course! I've looked at you, and I've been in a pool with you. You can *swim*, Maggie. You're a natural in the water!"

It was true. If there was any physical activity Maggie was any good at, swimming was it. Over the years, her mother had made sure of that by requesting summer afternoons off from her bookkeeping job to bring Maggie and Summer to the beach, where they took swimming lessons and spent more time in the water than onshore. Maggie knew all the strokes, from the crawl to the butterfly. To make present matters worse, after swimming lessons her mother joined Maggie and Summer in the water and, at their excited requests, taught them basic synchronized swimming moves. Maggie loved floating in that little circle, her toes just inches from her mother's and sister's. But she hadn't touched the water in two years, and this was most definitely not the time to jump back in.

"It could be so good for us, don't you think? An instant circle of friends, cute uniforms, lots of attention and exercise . . ."

"All fabulous reasons to try out." Maggie smiled. She really did think it was a great opportunity, for the right candidate.

Aimee leaned across the table and lowered her voice. "I know you probably think it's impossible, but really it's not. Tryouts are in a month. We have plenty of time to learn some choreography and practice in the water together. We don't even have to tell your mom until we've made the team."

Maggie looked across the cafeteria to where five members of the Water Wings sat by the windows, the streaming afternoon sunlight casting a warm, hazy glow around them, their makeup bags and their picked-at salads. Every now and then one or two of the members would toss their long hair back at something funny another member said, their movements slow and graceful, as though the stale cafeteria air were the pool water to which they were accustomed.

Maggie shook her head. "It's just not me. Solving logic proofs, conjugating French verbs, memorizing every state capital in the U.S.—that's me. That's what I do."

"But think about those college applications! The admissions people love an extracurricularly well-rounded person, don't they?"

"No fair!" Aimee knew how important getting accepted to college and receiving scholarships was to Maggie. Good grades and a full schedule of after-school activities were essential if she was going to have in the future all that she'd missed out on so far. "How do you have time for another team, anyway? Between volleyball, intramural soccer, and coaching girls' little league, your dance card should be full."

"The schedules work." Aimee shrugged and picked at her fruit salad. The glimmer faded from her eyes as she tried to spear an uncooperative grape.

"Aim?" Maggie asked when Aimee's lips set in a thin line.

"My parents told me last night that I can't *waste time* on another activity until my grades improve." When the pesky grape shot across the table, Aimee dropped her fork in defeat.

"Are they that bad? I thought you were coming in early for extra help."

When she shrugged again, Maggie sighed. Aimee had big plans for college too, but not via the academic route. They had the same classes and Maggie tried to help her study, but whenever they got together, Aimee always managed to change the subject.

Still, she knew better than anyone that parents didn't always know best. And she hated to see her friend down about anything. "I'll go to the pool with you," she finally offered. "I'll time you during laps to help you build up your endurance, I'll kneel on your feet if you want to do sit ups, but that's all I can do. I can help you do this, but not me." She poked at the dried cheese stuck to the corner of her plate and looked down. "I'm beyond help."

Before Aimee could deny the claim, Maggie spotted Peter Applewood and two other baseball players walking across the cafeteria toward the windows. Apparently she wasn't his only fan; both Anabel Richards and Julia Swanson snapped their compacts closed and pouted their lips at him instead of the minimirrors. Maggie watched Peter and his friends sit down with the Water Wings.

Maggie's stomach turned when Julia stood up from her seat to squeeze next to Peter. She thought she might lose her pizza as Julia tilted her head and gazed at him adoringly.

"Maggie, I think it would be a great thing for us to do together," Aimee said, snapping her back to reality. "But it's your decision. We have four weeks till tryouts. Take a week to think about it—for me, okay?"

Maggie gave Aimee a small smile, sorry to be disappointing her.

"And don't forget," Aimee added, "I wore reindeer antlers Christmas caroling at the South Street Senior Center, *and* stinky bowling shoes that had seen a thousand feet before mine for the charity tournament—for the happiness of other people's grandparents and our local animal shelters, yes, but also for *you*, Maggie."

Maggie smiled and nodded. She didn't think wearing reindeer antlers and bowling shoes for charitable causes was quite the same as wearing a bathing suit in front of strangers for sheer self-humiliation, but . . . "I'll think about it."

And she really would, because she owed it to Aimee and to the girl she wished she were: the pretty, fit one boys walked across crowded cafeteria floors for.

6. "Get ready, Mag Pie!"

Maggie finished the paragraph she'd been reading, slid her headphones around her neck, and glanced at the clock: 6:30 p.m. He was right on schedule.

"What for?" she asked casually.

He knocked on her door twice before pushing it open. "Your aunt will be here in fifteen minutes."

"Oh?" She reached for her earth science and social studies textbooks and brought them to her lap. "That's nice, but I don't think I'll have time to chat. I'm *really* busy."

Her father raised his eyebrows. "She's not coming to chat."

Maggie flipped open both books and scattered dozens of pages of notes around her. She rested her laptop on one knee and typed with her left hand as she highlighted random sentences in the earth science book with her right hand.

"Maggie?" He came all the way into the room. "It's Wednesday."

"Don't I know it!" She shook her head, looked up quickly, and gestured to her surroundings. "Looks like an all-nighter for me." The truth was she'd finished everything due through Friday the night before, but there was no way he'd know that.

"Well, it'll just have to wait." He crossed his arms over his chest. "You're going to Pound Patrollers with Aunt Violetta."

She lowered the highlighter and met his gaze. "Sorry, Dad, no can do. I have three tests, two papers, and a presentation tomorrow." She shrugged. "I'm swamped." She turned to her laptop, her heartbeat quickening.

"I know your studies are important."

She felt her muscles relax.

"But nothing is more important than your health."

She put the laptop on the floor, pushed the textbooks and papers from her lap, and stood up. "We'll just ask Mom. I'm sure she'll—"

"Your mother agrees, Maggie." He shifted slightly so that she couldn't fit past him through the door.

She stood with her hands on her hips. "I'm not going."

"Yes, you are. Aunt Violetta is on her way."

"I'll give her gas money and thank her for her time." She fanned her face with one hand as the heat began to spread.

"Drop the attitude, Maggie," he warned.

Her notebooks and laptop grew blurry as tears filled her eyes. "But, Dad, you don't understand," she pleaded. "What if I see someone I know? Or someone I don't know but who knows someone else I *do* know, and then people at school find out?" Forget the cool, calm, and collected plan. She wasn't above old-fashioned begging if it saved her from life-threatening embarrassment.

He cleared his throat and looked down. "I know it won't be easy, but it's for your own good."

Her mouth fell open. "But how do you *know*? No one even asked—"

"Maggie!" He held up one hand to stop her noisy blubbering. "We paid hard-earned, nonrefundable money for these meetings and you're going. End of story."

Silent tears zigzagged down her cheeks as she watched him leave her room and close the door. Money was such a sore household subject, he knew she'd never argue.

She sunk across the piles of notebook paper and highlighters that blanketed her bed, put on her headphones, turned up the volume, and covered her head with a pillow.

Instinctively she reached with one hand for the Snickers bag under her mattress.

By the time Maggie heard the doorbell ring exactly fifteen minutes later, she'd finished off the Snickers and begun working through a new bag of Twix.

Her parents had better be ready to raise her allowance. Her candy stash was going to need it.

7.

"Isn't this going to be so much fun?" Aunt Violetta squealed as they pulled out of the driveway.

Maggie tugged the hood of her sweatshirt over her head as her aunt started to whistle. She didn't know what reason her aunt had to be so happy, but the whistling lasted for twenty minutes and didn't stop until they reached the Pound Patrollers parking lot.

"Mag Pie." Aunt Violetta turned off the car and jumped out. "We don't want to miss the opening number, do we?"

"Opening number?" Maggie asked skeptically without looking away from the windshield. A group of teenagers had gathered in front of the adjacent pizzeria, and she sank in the seat, praying they weren't from her class.

"Yes, yes!" Aunt Violetta slapped her palm lightly on the

window. "You know, where we all get together in a circle and sing the club song!"

Maggie closed her eyes. Her parents were getting themselves into a fine mess very early on, because she planned on being very wealthy one day from her private medical practice, literary agency, or interior design company, and now she just couldn't be sure of future generosity.

"Aunt Violetta, is it okay if I stay in the car?" Maggie asked quietly, finally looking away from the windshield and leaning across the gearshift. She nodded her head in the direction of the teenagers, hoping her aunt would take pity on her. This would be so embarrassing that her already lame junior high experience could be shattered into a socially lifeless oblivion.

"What?" Aunt Violetta scrunched her nose and squinted at the teenagers. "Those buffoons?" She waved the idea away with one hand. "You'd have to wave pepperoni-covered video games in their faces to distract them from an upcoming meal."

Maggie slid so far down in her seat that she could no longer see through the windshield. She knew she was acting more childish than she ever had when it would've been more understandable and acceptable, like when she was five, but she just didn't care. She stomped her feet against the carpeted car floor and resisted the urge to bang her fists on the dashboard and scream loud and long enough to send the teenagers running home. Of course if she did any of these things, her next meeting would probably be in the psychiatric ward, courtesy of her loving parents.

She briefly wondered if the straightjacket would even fit.

"But, Aunt Violetta, I just don't think this place is for me," Maggie whispered, glancing at a pair of chubby dyed blondes walking together toward the Pound Patrollers door, their colorful rear ends bouncing into each other with every other step. "I mean, I'm so *young*."

Aunt Violetta inhaled deeply before sticking her head so far through the driver's side window, Maggie had to pull back to avoid a cranial collision.

"Sugarplum, I know this drives you crazy. Your family's a bundle of twigs, so what can *they* possibly know about *you*, huh?" She reached one hand through the window and laid it on Maggie's shoulder. "Fact is, sometimes young people are dealt some pretty bad cards in the game of life, cards worse than some adults will ever see. But I promise you, it just makes 'em better players. You can win this game, Mag Pie." She squeezed her shoulder.

"I don't want to *play*." Maggie sighed, slumped even farther down in the seat, and closed her eyes. She pictured herself sneaking into the pizza place, ducking into an oversize booth, and hiding behind a steaming pepperoni pie and a dozen garlic knots.

"Oh, for heaven's sake, grumpy pants!" Aunt Violetta finally sang, opening the passenger-side door so that Maggie had to drop her hand to the pavement to keep from falling out completely. "You might even have a tiny bit of fun if you just get over yourself! Let's go!"

"Cakes we like, cookies we love, and candy we adore, but cute clothes, feeling good, and being alive mean more!"

As if the club song weren't ridiculous enough, these nine women and one man stood in a circle, holding hands and swinging their arms above their heads, like the Whos in *How the Grinch Stole Christmas!* They stood around a tall scale, just like the one at Maggie's doctor's office—except for the fuchsia paint, silver cutouts of carrots, broccoli, and tomatoes, and streamers dangling from the balancing arm. Maggie hated scales—just the sight of them made her feel guilty about her last meal—but this one made her laugh behind her hands. Of course she hadn't yet been asked to step on it, and she had no intention of doing so if she was.

Aunt Violetta turned her head slightly during the humming portion of the song and nodded to Maggie to join the group, but Maggie stayed by the refreshment table of celery sticks, apple slices, and Dixie cups of water. She would've preferred hiding *under* the refreshment table, but feared that with her luck her rear end accidentally hitting the table would send snacks flying and foil her desired disappearing act.

"*So get up off your butt, say so long to your gut, and get out of that flabby rut . . . FOREVER!*"

The chubby circle squatted down and up out of imaginary chairs, waving plump fingers at their bellies before clapping and hugging one another. They all seemed as suspiciously happy as Aunt Violetta. Maggie picked up a celery stick and a water cup and sniffed each for a clue as to what sort of Pound Patrollers magical dietary supplement had sunk all of these people into weirdly cheerful states. Judging by their sizes, these were the ones who needed to pay for two airline seats or ask for seat belt extensions if they ever flew, who had to avoid the cramped booths at restaurants, and who couldn't help hogging both armrests at the movie theater. Without some sort of chemical assistance, how on earth could they be so happy?

"Whew! Well, okay then, let's all take our seats, shall we?" The leader of the group was a short, round redhead in a lime green velour tracksuit. She rolled the pink scale out of the way as the circle sat in oversize metal folding chairs.

Maggie squinted at the woman's name tag: ELECTRA.

Electra took a seat, clapped her hands together, and let out a small squeal. "So who'd like to start?"

Maggie's chin dropped when all nine members raised their arms. The only man in the group looked like he was in need of a bathroom break, the way he hopped and danced in his chair.

"Okay, Samuel, tell us about last week's goals." Electra nodded.

Samuel was suddenly still and inhaled so deeply that Maggie eventually peeked at her watch to time him. When he finally exhaled, the words came bouncing out of his mouth as though they'd all been jammed up, just waiting to be freed.

"Okay," he started, sitting up straight and patting his hands on his knees, "we all know about the new Krispy Kreme up on Grove and Market—"

Groans and head shaking took over the circle. Maggie knew the store exactly, and had been there for the grand opening of the hottest, sweetest donuts ever created.

"—and when we met last week I'd said how I was having a *really* hard time not stopping in before work and picking up a half dozen for the *office* and eating every single one myself before the midmorning meeting. I couldn't resist the glowing red light telling me they were fresh out of the oven and still hot!" He paused and waved one hand in front of his face, needing to cool down after such a thought.

The women in the circle nodded in unison, completely understanding Samuel's predicament.

"Well, I decided that my goal for last week would be to start small and allow just one donut each morning, so long as I didn't lie to myself or anyone else about whom the treat was really for. That way I wasn't quitting cold turkey, because let's face it, that wasn't going to happen, but I was eliminating about one thousand five hundred unnecessary sugar calories!"

Samuel hesitated and looked around at the women, who eagerly looked back, awaiting his story's finale.

"And?" Electra finally prompted.

"And"—Samuel clapped his hands together one time— "I did it! Thursday, Friday, Monday, and Tuesday mornings, I had only one glazed donut each, and this morning, I was running late and decided to forego the trip, and forgot all about what I thought I'd freak out about missing!"

The women erupted in applause and cheers, and Maggie half expected them to leap out of their seats and bombard him with hugs and pats on the back.

"Just wonderful," Electra said as the clapping quieted,

shaking her head as she marveled at Samuel's achievement.

The group nodded their heads approvingly. From where she stood, Maggie could see Samuel mouthing silent thank-yous to the circle of women.

"Now, why did Samuel have such success with his goal this week?"

"He cut himself back, instead of cutting himself off," an older woman with a long silvery braid offered.

Electra slapped one knee. "Exactly! Like we've talked about before, eating better doesn't mean you have to give up everything you love about food, it just means you have to think about what you're doing and try to make better decisions."

As the group members quietly discussed Samuel's progress among themselves and Electra made notes on a plastic blue clipboard, Maggie observed them from her safe position in the back of the room, noting with satisfaction that no one there was like her. Nobody else was even *near* her age. What could they possibly have in common, besides a love of food?

Her muscles relaxed as she noted the differences between herself and everyone else, and she leaned against the folding table, reached behind her for a cup of water, and brought it to her lips. Only forty minutes to go—she could do it.

"What a bunch of wackos, huh?" a voice whispered next to her.

The water she'd just sipped caught in her throat and her eyes filled with tears. She tried to keep the liquid from shooting out of her nose, looked to the ceiling, fanned her face with one hand, and finally swallowed.

"Arnie, as in Arnold, as in Schwarzenegger."

Maggie looked down at the extended hand and up to the round face that smiled at her and nearly choked again, even though her throat was dry.

"As in *Terminator*? *Kindergarten Cop*? Future United States President?" He raised one eyebrow when she didn't respond.

But what could she say? She'd *just* calmed down upon realizing that this meeting was most definitely not where she belonged. And now here stood Arnie, in baggy cargo pants, an oversize sweatshirt, and a red knit cap.

Arnie, another preteen Pound Patroller.

8. "Well, all right, sugarplum. Next week, same time, same place, righto?" Aunt Violetta hollered out of the car window.

Maggie waved quickly before hurrying up the front steps. She paused, listened to the television through the wall, and silently pressed her forehead against the cool wood of the door. Coming home was just never as warm and fuzzy an event as it was in the movies and on television. And she'd only been returning to this home for six months, since the first item on her father's agenda after losing his job had been to move into a smaller house to save on rent.

She closed her eyes, gently tapped her forehead against the door three times, and told herself there was no place like home, even though the biggest and brightest pair of ruby slippers couldn't have convinced her.

Her dad was in his usual spot, on their faded floral couch in jeans and a flannel shirt, tapping the remote control on one knee and rubbing his bare feet together as though he hadn't a care in the world.

"Hey, kiddo."

She waved halfheartedly and hurried past him before he could ask questions she didn't feel like answering.

The one person she did want to talk to was her mother, but she wasn't in any of her usual places, on the phone or reading in the kitchen or her bedroom.

She flung open her door without looking up and kicked off her sneakers. She was rummaging through her dresser drawers for an oversize nightshirt when she noticed something move in the mirror above her head. Yelping when the drawer accidentally closed on her thumbs, she grabbed a hairbrush in self-defense and spun around.

"Mom?" Maggie asked, confused. She might've scolded her mother for the invasion of privacy, but she looked so small lying on Maggie's bed, cradling a stuffed moose with her eyes closed.

Maggie let the hairbrush fall to her side and forgot the throbbing in her thumbs.

Her mother was curled up on one side, the stuffed moose in her arms and Maggie's purple comforter draped loosely across her legs. She wore jeans and a white sweater, her long, dark brown hair up in a messy ponytail, a usual postwork ensemble. But her face looked darker, sadder, and Maggie realized her mother wasn't wearing her signature red lipstick, the same kind she applied before kissing napkins for Summer's lunchboxes or notes left on the kitchen counter. The lipstick she wore because "You never know who you're going to meet!"

"Mom?" Maggie asked again.

Finally her mother's eyes snapped open. Seeing Maggie standing beside her, she sat straight up and threw the comforter off of her legs.

"Sweetie, hi, how was the meeting?" She tightened her ponytail and straightened her sweater as though nothing out of the ordinary had happened.

"What?" Pound Patrollers now seemed to be a months-old embarrassment. Maggie shook her head. "Fine, but what are you doing in here?"

Her mother patted the bed and looked around, as though the answer were hidden in one of the Monet posters dotting the walls or in the notes and textbooks still scattered at the foot of the bed. She stood up and flapped her hand once in front of her face, dismissing her presence as anything abnormal.

"I was just bringing your clean clothes up." She gestured toward the floor, where Maggie's pajama bottoms, socks, underwear, and T-shirts were strewn about, like her dirty clothes usually were before making it to the wash. "And I just got suddenly tired, so I lay down for a bit. That's all." She kissed the top of Maggie's head before gathering the clothes and quickly refolding them into a neat pile on top of the dresser.

"So, I'm going to go start dinner. I'll see you in a bit." And she hurried out of the room before Maggie could remind her that it was eight thirty and they'd eaten three hours before.

After Maggie watched her mother go in and out of the kitchen and then into the bathroom, she picked up the fallen moose from the floor. Her father had given one to her and one to Summer during their last family vacation to New Hampshire, where there'd seemed to be more yellow signs warning of moose crossing than actual moose. They'd never spotted one, but her father had slowed down for every rock and shrub, just in case.

Maggie rested the moose next to her pillow, cleared her textbooks, notes, and laptop from the bed, and changed into her pajamas. Too tired to update her completed assignments on the Master Multitasker spreadsheet and too mortified to finish off the Twix she'd opened earlier, she crawled into bed and turned off the light.

When her head landed on something hard, she turned the light back on and reached under the pillow.

Her mother's leather photo album.

Maggie leaned against the wall and brought the album to her lap. She hadn't let anyone take her picture in months, but these photos were from the year before. She turned the pages slowly, examining each as though it contained clues. In them, she wore a size twelve instead of a size eighteen, Summer turned cartwheels in their old backyard, her mother baked cookies, and her father posed proudly next to his company truck.

She paused at her father's picture. She'd forgotten that smile. He'd worked for the same landscaper for years, and had gotten the truck right after his boss had promised him eventual partnership. They'd all piled in and he'd driven them past the yards of the company's biggest clients, promising to one day buy them their very own house with their very own perfect lawn.

The layoff came unexpectedly two months later. Budget cuts, his boss had said.

Maggie sighed, closed the album, and exchanged it for her laptop on the floor. Settling back against the wall, she brought the stuffed New Hampshire moose next to her and opened the laptop.

When the Master Multitasker glowed in front of her, she clicked on "Miscellaneous" and added a new item above the original three.

#1: FIND DAD A JOB.

She couldn't wait to check it off.

9. "All righty, girly girls. Softball's the name of the game today and if anyone gives me any lip-glossed lip about cramps, bloating, or PMS-related physically impairing moodiness, it's laps around the track for the next six weeks!" Ms. Pinkerton yelled into her new megaphone.

Maggie and Aimee looked at each other and rolled their eyes as several girls around them covered their ears and winced.

"I didn't think *any*thing could be more annoying than the whistle," Aimee whispered.

"Ooh, ooh, Ms. Pinkerton!" Genevieve Snodgrass waved one French manicured hand in the air. "I'd love to be a captain!"

Ms. Pinkerton snorted into the megaphone.

"Nobody wants a whiner for a captain, missy! Now get in line with everyone else!"

Maggie would rather play softball than run around the track any day, but the game definitely had its own low points, some of which occurred well before the first pitch. Two years ago, she was considered an average softball player—not *good*, but good enough to get picked by the captains somewhere in the middle of the team-forming process. She could usually hit two out of three pitches—not *far*, but usually far enough to get to first base. But these days she just couldn't move her legs fast enough to beat the ball to the first baseman's glove. So while her hits were still decent, they were about as effective as a strikeout or an easily caught fly ball, making her a less-than-desired teammate.

Genevieve Snodgrass could barely wrap her fingers around the bat because of her perfectly done nails, but she could at least shuffle down the baseline on tiptoes faster than Maggie could sprint.

"Anabel and Julia, you're up!"

Maggie bit her lip, disappointed. For some reason, she still had faith that adults, especially teachers, believed in equal opportunities. If Julia and Anabel were already captains of *something* on a daily basis and enjoying all the emotional and social benefits, couldn't this opportunity be shared with non–Water Wings?

Anabel and Julia stepped away from the line and turned to face them. Maggie unconsciously crossed her arms over her stomach upon being confronted with two sets of toned arms, flat tummies, and defined quadriceps. They stood with their hands on their hips, legs shoulder-width apart, and identical green bubbles growing from their perfect, pink-frosted lips.

"Remember!" Ms. Pinkerton bellowed. "It's not rocket science, and it's not a stinkin' popularity contest! You want runners and hitters if you want to win, and if you don't want to win, go home and stop wasting my time!" She stepped to the side but kept the megaphone raised and her forefinger curled around the small black button, ready to fire.

Anabel snapped her gum. "Mandy," she called to the tallest, fastest runner in the class.

"Becca," Julia called out to the second tallest, fastest runner in the class.

Mandy and Becca stepped behind their captains, exchanging energetic high fives.

"Aimee," Anabel announced next.

Maggie patted her friend on the back as she jogged over to her new team. Aimee was always one of the first five chosen, and Maggie couldn't wait for the day that she graduated to captain, because surely she'd pick Maggie somewhat sooner than anyone else would.

And so it went, name after name until the only two remaining were Maggie and Gretchen, a pale, pint-size girl with arms as thick and strong as cooked spaghetti noodles and eyeglasses as thick and strong as the tree trunk they both tried to hide behind. They were probably equally athletic, but Gretchen had at least the chance of being successfully whisked away and carried by the wind to first base, should she hit the ball.

Maggie closed her eyes momentarily, prepared to be the last one chosen—again. What was so wrong with assigning teams before class? Or dividing up alphabetically?

The girls were quiet, waiting for Julia to make her final selection.

"Julia!" Ms. Pinkerton megaphoned when Julia remained silent and turned to face the rest of her teammates.

She jumped. "What?" she snapped accidentally before turning back around and facing in the direction of the remaining girls. "Maggie," she called, and glanced at Ms. Pinkerton. "Sorry, I thought she knew."

Being picked last meant that her name usually wasn't even called, because it was just automatically assumed that she would join whichever team hadn't just chosen, so that it wasn't even Maggie the individual being picked last, but some nameless, useless player. But she hadn't been picked last this time, and she wondered why Julia thought she'd know to join her team.

Too happy to worry about it, Maggie smiled in spite of herself and waved in consolation to Gretchen before walking over to her new team.

As Gretchen began the lonely walk across the patch of dirt separating her from the rest of the girls, Maggie saw Julia's mouth drop open.

"But, Ms. Pinkerton, I didn't see anyone else standing there!"

"What're you complaining about, Swanson?" Ms. Pinkerton shouted into the megaphone, even though she'd already rejoined the group.

"Gretchen! I didn't see Gretchen standing there!"

"So what? You have your team, Richards has hers. Let's play ball!"

"No, but Ms. Pinkerton, I absolutely would've picked Gretchen over Maggie if I'd *seen* her!"

"Were you sleeping?"

"No!" Julia shook her head.

"Sun in your eyes? Shiny, green bubbles cloud your vision?"

"No, Ms. Pinkerton. I just don't think I saw her past Maggie, is all!" Julia declared.

Maggie heard Aimee gasp from her place in the crowd. The rest of the girls grew suddenly quiet and though Maggie looked down at her sneakers, she felt the eyes of the less considerate girls turn slightly to see her reaction. Her smile had disappeared and she searched her brain (unsuccessfully) for some way to joke about the situation.

After seven seconds that felt like seven hours standing naked in the middle of a New Year's Eve Times Square with her image plastered on electronic billboards for all to see, Maggie was finally released by Ms. Pinkerton clearing her throat into the megaphone.

"These are the teams. Bats are to your left, gloves are to your right, Richards is in the field, and, Swanson, ready your hitters!"

"Sorry, Maggie," Julia mumbled, not meeting Maggie's eyes or pausing for a response before hurrying toward the bats.

No one was looking, but Maggie shrugged anyway, because she thought she deserved to have a reaction. As her team lined up behind home plate and the other team scrambled across the diamond and outfield, Maggie squeezed into the dugout and crossed her fingers for a long three outs.

10.

"Two more to go!" Maggie called to Aimee, who cut through the pool water with unhurried, smooth strokes and a smile every time she turned her face for air.

Aimee gave a quick thumbs-up before pushing against the wall and turning upside down and around underwater.

While she made her way to the other side, Maggie bent over to roll up her pant legs. There was no way she'd actually go swimming, but afternoon sunlight streamed through the glass ceiling, music played from the overhead speakers, and all she needed was a fruity drink with a little umbrella to convince her she was on a tropical vacation and not just at the school pool. Dangling her legs in the water just might be reason enough to write a postcard home.

She frowned when her right pant leg stopped midcalf.

Rather than grab the material with both hands and force it over her flesh, she quickly lowered both cuffs to just above her ankles, sank quickly to the ground, and patted the water with her bare feet, as though that was what she'd intended all along.

Aimee's blue-cap-covered head broke the water's surface, sending cool droplets flying through the air and onto Maggie's arms. Maggie happily showed her the stopwatch that announced a five-second improvement from the day before.

Aimee slapped the water and laughed before throwing her cap and goggles out of the pool and dunking back her long blond hair.

"Your turn!" She reached up and grabbed Maggie's foot.

Maggie pulled back. "Oops, I just happened to forget my swimsuit at home. Again."

Aimee rolled her eyes and spun around in the water. "Mags, we're the only ones here."

"No, we're not."

"Yes, we are. The after-school elementary kids are gone, water polo practice is over, and the dive team is at an away meet. It's just us!"

Maggie shook her head and nodded toward the opposite end of the pool.

"Aqua Adam? That silly excuse for a lifeguard? He hasn't looked up from his BMX magazine in twenty minutes!" Aimee exclaimed. "You could leap from the diving board onto his lap and he wouldn't raise an eyebrow, let alone a whistle."

"First of all, I couldn't *leap* if I wanted to. The best I can do on my own is hop. Second of all, even if some magical, unexplained physics phenomenon happened to occur at the exact moment I left the diving board to send me flying into his lap, the poor boy wouldn't raise an eyebrow because of sudden paralysis!"

Aimee rolled her eyes and held out one hand. "Give me the stopwatch."

"You'll get it wet."

"It's water-resistant," Aimee said, hand still extended.

"I'm not getting in the pool—"

"I know you're not getting in the pool, just give it to me, please."

Maggie bit her lip and rested the stopwatch in Aimee's hand.

"Thank you. Now, on the count of three, name three things that happened this week that made you feel as cool and carefree as you'd feel in this pool. If you can't name three things in less than sixty seconds, you'll swim with me tomorrow afternoon."

"And if I can?"

"I'll buy a beach chair with a built-in cup holder for you to sit in while I practice."

"Aimee, what on earth are you trying—"

"One!"

"This is really very silly—"

"Two!"

"What is this going to—"

"Three! Go!"

As Aimee clicked the stopwatch, Maggie leaned back on her hands and tried to recall good things of the past week. She wouldn't have humored anyone else, but Maggie knew Aimee had a point and she'd let her make it. Still, the simple sound of the stopwatch clicking start made her heartbeat quicken and her palms moisten. Whatever the point was, it'd better be good.

"Well," she began, raising one hand for emphasis, "I talked to Peter the other day—"

"When he found your book in his locker?" Aimee asked quickly, not looking up from the stopwatch.

"Yes."

"Were you more embarrassed than happy?"

"Yes."

"Doesn't count."

"Okay, well, I was happy when the social studies test was over on Monday." Maggie knew it was a lame thing to be happy about, but she'd studied all weekend for it.

"Happy, or relieved?"

"Both?" Maggie asked, raising her eyebrows.

Aimee rolled her eyes. "Fine, that's one. Next?"

Maggie looked up to the glass roof of the natatorium. The sky was beginning to darken, just like her brain, apparently, when she tried to search it for happy moments of the past week. Much to her embarrassment, she kept picturing the Snickers under her bed or the double-chocolate Betty Crocker brownies her mom had made the night before, and she couldn't tell Aimee that, even though the chocolate had still been soft and warm when she'd smuggled two extra brownies into her room after dinner. The only other thing she could think of was Pound Patrollers, an experience so mortifying that she'd vowed not to tell *anyone*—not even Aimee—and to pretend like it never happened. She wished there was more to remember, like that she'd gotten asked to the movies or bought a cute dress that actually fit her or lost ten pounds. Or twenty pounds. Or thirty.

"Ten!" Aimee announced.

"Okay, well." Maggie shook her head. There had to be *something* else. Two out of three wouldn't be so bad.

"Five!"

Hadn't anyone said anything nice to her? Given her a compliment? Hadn't she managed to come out of her head and stomach long enough to feel good about something she'd said or done? Had there been no A plusses to be proud of this week?

"Time!" Aimee smiled and tossed the stopwatch back to Maggie before raising herself out of the pool.

"Don't worry, I'll call you in the morning to remind you about your swimsuit," Aimee said triumphantly, grabbing a towel and ignoring Maggie's protests as they headed toward the locker room.

11.

"I'm staying after school tomorrow," Maggie announced brightly, passing Summer the bowl of peas and carrots.

Summer passed the bowl to their mother, who passed it to their father. Maggie watched this exchange and waited for someone to acknowledge her comment, but no one even looked up.

Maggie tapped her knife on the Tupperware salad bowl. "Hello?" she asked, raising her eyebrows.

Her father lowered his head closer to his plate and shoveled food into his mouth.

"What's that, honey?" her mother finally asked.

"I'm staying after school," Maggie repeated with a sigh, "tomorrow."

"Well, that's nice," her mother said without meeting Maggie's eyes.

That's *nice*? Her mother was the biggest encourager of extracurricular activities, always asking when something would meet, how often, who was in charge, who were the members, when could she come to watch, and not out of parental nosiness, but of sincere interest.

"What is it?" Summer asked brightly.

Maggie flashed a grateful smile. "It's a new thing I'm thinking of trying," she said casually, hoping to fuel further questions. She was so nervous about getting in the pool that she normally wouldn't have even considered mentioning it, but everyone had been so tense lately that she thought her news might make for good distraction.

"That's wonderful, sweetie." Her mother smiled briefly at her before returning her eyes to her plate.

Maggie bit her lip. Looked from her mother to her father. Something was up.

"It's not just any old thing, either," she tried one more time. "It's not even *academic*." That should get them, if nothing else.

"Is it a club? Or an after-school job?" Summer's voice was unnaturally loud as she tried to snap their parents out of silence.

Her father reached into his jeans pocket and pulled out the television remote. The house was so small that the living room television could be turned on from just about anywhere, and before Maggie could say anything else, Alex Trebek joined them for dinner.

Maggie finished her meatloaf and peas and carrots in silence, annoyed at her family's apathy, but not angry. Something was going on that she didn't know about. She cleared her plate with Summer finishing close behind, put both plates in the dishwasher, and retreated to the safety of her room.

A quarter of the way through her earth science reading, Maggie was unintentionally informed.

When she heard her mother's muffled voice trickle underneath the bedroom door, she got up from her desk and crouched with one ear in the direction of the living room, her heart pounding. It had been at least three days since the last argument, so they were due.

"I can't believe you didn't go," her mother said, in disbelief. "*Why* wouldn't you go?"

"So I missed the appointment. Big deal. There are plenty of others."

"Plenty of others? When? Where?"

"I know what I'm doing."

"If that's the case, why are we having this conversation?"

Maggie nibbled her fingernails.

"The job thing isn't the problem—"

"No, Robert, the problem is that they're going to turn off the lights and disconnect the phone because we haven't paid those bills in two months!"

"Everything looks better in the dark and there's nobody I need to talk to."

"And *rent*, Robert. Rent was due two weeks ago! We're already going to have to pay a late fee, just like we've had to the past three months, and last time Mrs. Morgan said that if it kept happening—"

"She's not going to kick us out."

Her mother sighed and Maggie pictured her holding her forehead with both hands, the way she did when it seemed her brain might explode from stress.

"Robert. Mrs. Morgan depends on this money to live. *We* depend on money to live"—her mother sighed—"besides the fact that I had to beg my uncle for that interview. Couldn't you have at least talked to him?"

The silence that followed was so loud, Maggie could've put on her headphones with the stereo volume cranked to ten and still strained to hear the music.

She looked at the clock. Four minutes passed before her mother spoke again, her voice softer.

"Robert, I know it was a shock, losing your job so unexpectedly, but I'm tired. I need help. I can't keep asking my parents for money."

"If your uncle was so willing to contribute to our cause, why don't you ask him?"

Maggie heard her mother's sudden hurried footsteps around the house. The familiar clinking of glasses and plates in the kitchen let Maggie know her mother was keeping busy to deal, the way she always did, while her father sat nearby, maybe feeling badly about the argument's turn but unwilling to make it better. He'd never been a very emotional person, but since losing his job, he'd become about as sensitive as a rock.

Maggie crawled into bed and drew the covers over her head. She reached one hand underneath the bed and grabbed the first plastic bag her fingers grazed, pleased when it was the Kit Kats. She ate one after another, the chocolate melting as quickly and easily as the harsh sentences flew out of her parents' mouths.

She thought of dinner at Aimee's house, during which the McDougall family actually talked about everything—their days, friends, and upcoming events. They asked questions and even lingered at the table when everyone was done eating, and laughed at one another's stories. The television was nowhere near the dining room table; in fact Maggie couldn't recall ever seeing the McDougalls watch television. After dinner the kids cleaned up, and later everyone ate dessert together on comfy couches in front of the living room fireplace. In the winter Maggie and Aimee did their homework by that fireplace after school with cups of hot chocolate and real whipped cream. Aimee's whole house was something right out of a Pottery Barn catalog, which featured beautiful furniture and household items on pages that Maggie's mom earmarked, but from which she never actually bought a thing.

The McDougall house wasn't just a house. It was a home. A warm, safe, happy place to return to at the end of the day—just like on television or in the movies.

Maggie finished off the bag of Kit Kats, licked her fingers, and lifted her laptop from the floor. When Maggie's Master Multitasker appeared, she inserted a new tab on the bottom of the screen and labeled it "Dad." She typed quickly, as though the faster the ideas came, the sooner things would go back to normal.

#1: Get newspaper for job listings.

#2: Look for help wanted signs.

#3: See if other landscaping companies are hiring.

She studied the list, grabbed a peppermint patty from

her nightstand drawer to help her think, and added one last item.

#4: Make Dad *want* a new job.

She saved the changes, closed the laptop, and lowered it to the floor. She lay down, pulled the covers to her chin, and was about to put on her headphones when she heard a light knock on her door.

Thinking she misheard, Maggie kicked off the covers and sat straight up in her bed. There it was again.

She stood up, unlocked the door, and cracked it open.

A small pair of sad brown eyes stared back at her.

"They're fighting again."

Maggie leaned against the door. "Do you want to be the car?"

Summer nodded.

Maggie opened the door all the way, gave Summer the headphones to block out any potential noise, and pulled Monopoly from the closet. They moved the car and thimble game pieces around the board without talking until Summer fell asleep on a pile of pink, green, and blue bills.

12. "You promise?" Aimee asked skeptically, one palm on the swinging locker room door.

Maggie swallowed and nodded.

"You're not going to turn right around as soon as I get in and hightail it home?"

"I'm in my *bathing* suit," Maggie defended herself. "I'm not going anywhere but underwater where no one can see me. I just need a minute—or five, tops."

"Fine. Just remember the reindeer antlers and stinky bowling shoes. Consider me your favorite charity." Aimee winked before pushing through the door.

It's no big deal, she told herself, clinging to the yellow striped towel she'd brought from home (not trusting the small white school towels to wrap all the way around her).

It's just a bathing suit. Every person out there is already wearing one.

Peering through the door's window, she waited for the dive team to finish stretching and move toward the diving platforms before taking a deep breath and throwing open the door. Her feet were slippery on the tiles but she didn't look or slow down. Staring straight ahead at the water, she padded along as quickly as she could before dropping her towel, hurrying to sit on the edge of the pool, and sliding in. She hoped she'd looked more graceful than she'd felt, shuffling and waddling like a beached seal, but she looked casually around once safely in the water and was relieved to find no one gaping or laughing. No one was even paying attention, except Aimee, who smiled before dunking underwater and swimming over to Maggie.

"You did it! The worst part is over."

"*One* of the worst parts is over," Maggie corrected. "I still have to get out!"

Aimee dismissed the thought with a wave of her hand. "So what do you want to do first? Breaststroke? Backstroke? Crawl? Handstands?"

Maggie's eyes widened and she shook her head at the last option. "*Under*water! That's part of the deal!"

After agreeing on free swim, they moved over to one wall and grabbed the ledge, braced for push off. Maggie knew she wasn't competing against Aimee, but lined up against the wall she felt she was competing against someone or something—she just wasn't sure who or what.

They pushed off at the same time and Maggie let herself glide through the water for a few seconds, enjoying the cool rush against her skin, before beginning to kick and paddle. She hadn't really swum in years, but it seemed to be like riding a bicycle, as the strokes came easily.

"Doing okay?" Aimee asked, popping up for air after another underwater turnaround.

"I feel like we should be surrounded by hammocks and palm trees!"

Aimee grinned, gave a goggled wink, and swam ahead.

It *did* feel like vacation. With each cut her arms made though the water, Maggie relaxed more. Jimmy Buffett's "Margaritaville" played from the overhead speakers and the sun warmed her arms each time they left the water. Her movements were unhurried but steady. When her arms grew tired, instead of worrying about how out of shape she was, she simply rolled over and did the backstroke. She moved through the water slowly and gracefully, her breathing and movements even, her head clear. She didn't think about how she looked or who was around, about how her bathing suit straps tightened around her shoulders with each motion, or about her parents, Peter Applewood, Water Wings, Ms. Pinkerton, or Pound Patrollers.

"*This* is exercise?" Maggie called to Aimee as they swam past each other.

She'd never thought of swimming as a workout. But her muscles contracted and her heart pumped, so even without the familiar cramping and sore calves, she knew her body was working.

They swam for a half an hour before Maggie began to tire. She flagged Aimee down and waited for her on one side of the shallow end.

"So, you know better than anybody that I hate being wrong," Maggie said with a smile as Aimee swam over. "But I was very wrong, and you were very, very right. This was amazing."

It was the first time she'd felt lighter than a hippopotamus in months. She'd decided on the fifth turnaround that temporary weightlessness was enough to pursue a career in swimming or aeronautics; whether in the water or on the moon, defying gravity was the professional goal for her.

"I knew it!" Aimee dunked herself quickly underwater and popped back up. "So that means you'll come again, right?"

Maggie grinned. "Is tomorrow too soon? And the day after tomorrow? And the day after that?"

Once Aimee released Maggie's neck from her excited squeeze, they rested their elbows behind them on the edge of the pool and let their legs float in front of them.

"So I know I probably shouldn't ask you so soon, but time *is* sort of running out."

Maggie turned her head to look at her friend. "Running out? What for?" This afternoon Maggie had felt she had all the time in the world.

"For the Water Wings tryouts?" Aimee asked timidly.

Maggie sighed. "Aim, I just got in the water. I don't know if I'm quite ready for everyone to watch me try to move around in it."

"But you're a natural, Mags! You swim like you were born doing it. It's just another thing that you're good at, like algebra or memorizing state capitals."

Maggie bit her lip, tasted the chlorine. It wasn't chocolate, but it somehow tasted sweeter. Could she really do it? Was joining a water sport team *not* completely out of character? Was it only out of the character she thought she was?

"Mom only taught me basic, ancient moves. I don't know any of the choreography," Maggie protested weakly with her last concern, her heart beginning to beat faster and a small smile forming.

Aimee snapped her head around to look at Maggie. "I'll teach you the routine to try out with, and they teach you the rest after you've made the team."

After you've made the team.

"Okay."

Aimee paused, her lips widening in a disbelieving grin. "Okay?"

"I'll do it." Maggie squeezed her eyes shut and shook her head, disbelieving it herself. She was so excited and distracted that she actually climbed the silver ladder without one glance around to see if anyone watched. "On one condition," she added over her shoulder.

"Anything," Aimee agreed, planting both palms on the pool's edge and hoisting herself out.

"You let me help you study." She wanted Aimee to have better grades, but if by some otherworldly bizarre phenomenon Maggie actually made the team, she also wanted to ensure she wasn't joining it alone. And Aimee's parents had already forbidden more activities unless her grades improved.

Wrinkling her nose, Aimee leaned over to wring water from her hair.

"It's good ammo for your disapproving parents," Maggie suggested.

"They *do* think you're an academic goddess," Aimee admitted reluctantly.

"Well." Maggie shrugged and smiled.

"Okay, *fine*," Aimee groaned. "It's only fair."

"See? You're a quick learner!"

"Anyway," Aimee said, the excitement back in her voice as she headed toward the locker room, "we have to come up with some sort of practice schedule for the next three weeks, and maybe we should go bathing suit shopping so that we stand out and—"

Aimee stopped her quick walk to the locker room when she noticed Maggie was no longer behind her. She looked over her shoulder to see her friend stuck by the water's edge, stiff and wet like a defenseless statue in the rain, and then up to the bleachers, from where she heard hushed whispers and muffled snorts of laughter.

Anabel Richards and Julia Swanson sat on one of the benches, giggling and peeking above the hands that covered their mouths. They shone in their silver bathing suits, which they wore without cover-ups, looking like they'd just slithered off the pages of a Victoria's Secret catalog, each fixing her hair with one hand and hiding her smirk with the other.

And if that wasn't enough to embarrass Maggie into a catatonic state, on the bleacher right behind them sat Peter Applewood.

Maggie stood at the pool's edge, frozen. She looked down at her toes without seeing them, brought her knees together, bent over slightly, and crossed her arms over her stomach, trying without thinking to curl into a shell of herself and hide. She didn't know how long they'd been sitting there, but guessed it was long enough to have heard the Water Wings discussion, which only worsened the trauma of being so blatantly scrutinized in her skirted bathing suit. She turned her head slightly to see her striped yellow towel sitting in a sad lump at least six feet away. To retrieve it quickly she'd have to turn around and reveal her butt, which resembled a cottage cheese-filled Jell-O mold in bright packaging. The only other option was to get back in the water, which she couldn't do for fear of her splash fueling further laughter.

So she stood in one place, water dripping from her hair and bathing suit and her toes threatening to stick permanently to the poolside tile.

She raised her eyes slightly when she heard Aimee's bare feet pattering across the tile to the striped towel and then over to Maggie. She stood up straighter once the towel was wrapped around her and shuffled as quickly as she could without slipping and falling (the only possible way the situation could be worse) toward the locker room door.

"Hey, nice dress!" Julia called before erupting into hysterics with Anabel.

"What's your problem?"

Maggie glanced quickly over her shoulder to see Aimee standing in front of Anabel and Julia, hands on her hips.

"Come on," Julia said, her voice still light with laughter. "It was funny."

Had Maggie stuck around, she might've noticed that Peter didn't join in their amusements, but sat silently, shaking his head not at Maggie but at her two silver-suited antagonists. And had she stuck around and actually turned around, she would've witnessed the swift shove he threw at Julia's shoulder that turned her laughter into a surprised yelp before he got up and left the pool alone.

But she didn't stick around. She made it to the locker room without falling, threw her school clothes on over her soaked bathing suit, and ran as fast as her legs would carry her toward home, her bed, and the covers she would hide under until she'd withered away to practically nothing and was light enough that someone could actually drag her out if they tried—if they even thought to look, which Maggie doubted they would.

13.

Maggie pressed one ear against the bathroom door. Her father watched television while her mother helped Summer with her homework. Their voices were soft, which meant they were down the hall.

The coast was clear.

She lifted the scale from the floor and slid it under her sweatshirt, wincing when the cool metal pressed against her belly. She held the scale in place with one hand and rested the other on the doorknob. Satisfied that her family was too busy to pay attention, she slipped through the door, dashed down the hall to her bedroom, and locked herself inside.

Maggie hadn't touched a scale since her last school physical. She liked having her height measured, because she felt her five-foot-seven frame helped rationalize her weight. But during the actual weighing, she always looked away from the long, narrow bar and asked the nurse to record the result without sharing and quickly slide both weights back to zero.

But she had no choice now. There was no one there to absorb the bad news for her, and the mortifying pool incident had convinced her she needed to know the truth.

She twisted the doorknob to make sure she was locked safely inside and, more importantly, that her family was locked safely outside. Because clothes, especially *her* clothes, would negatively skew the scale's reading, the truth involved getting naked.

She closed her eyes, took three deep breaths, and slowly unzipped her sweatshirt, cringing and biting her lip harder and harder with the revealing of each flabby roll.

She tugged on one sleeve and then the other till the heavy gray sweatshirt fell to the blue bathroom tile. She lifted the Camp Sound View T-shirt that her mother had brought back as a souvenir from Summer's day camp two years before, which was just a reminder of how silly *Maggie* would've felt at camp, playing volleyball and going canoeing. The only camp she was fit for was the annual Pound Patrollers "retreat," which took place in the local mall. Campers walked six brisk lengths, from the Gap to JCPenney and back again, before indulging in low-fat, all-natural fruit smoothies at the food court, every morning, from Memorial Day through Labor Day. Aunt Violetta had done the retreat for so many summers that she'd already applied for leader-in-training, even though the next session wouldn't start again for eight months.

Maggie reached behind her and unhooked her bra, the boring, beige cotton racerback that lacked any cute polka dots, ruffles, lace, bows, or satin—small details that might've helped her feel more like a girl than just a body with mushy parts that needed extra restraining.

She sighed and watched the beige bra drop to the floor.

She was naked except for her underwear and debated stepping onto the scale with them on (because how much could boring, frill-free cotton possibly weigh?), before deciding it was no time to take chances.

She hooked her thumbs on the waistband of her boring beige cotton briefs (as in grandma-style, not bikini, hip hugger, low rider, or, heaven forbid, thong) and gently tugged them over her stomach and thighs. She briefly wondered if the lingerie gods smiled down at her for at least wearing a matching set, but then decided that the cotton lumps probably didn't even qualify as lingerie. They were undergarments. "Panties" was too delicate a term. Even "underwear" seemed too risqué. "Undergarments" was just about boring enough.

So, there she was, naked—in her birthday suit, without anyone giving her presents or feeding her cake to make the experience worthwhile. Naked, in her bedroom on a random Tuesday night. She looked down and just barely saw her toenails peeking out from the shadow of her stomach.

Her heart pounded so loudly that she was sure her dad heard it over Alex Trebek and *Jeopardy!*, and her palms were so moist that she had to keep patting them on her bedspread. She brushed her hair away from her face, closed her eyes, and slowly stepped one foot onto the scale, then the other, wincing when the metal gave slightly. She inhaled for five one-one thousands, and exhaled for ten. When it seemed her lungs might turn inside out, she finally opened her eyes.

And almost fell off the scale.

186.

She peered over her belly, squinted to make sure she read the numbers correctly. She leaned to one side, then the other. Tilted forward, then backward. The skinny black dial quivered but stuck to its initial estimate.

Her heart booming in her ears, she backed off and away from the scale until she felt the cool doorknob against her bare skin.

Maggie inched back toward the metal box and hoped that when she looked down again the scale would read twenty or thirty, instead of zero. Such an inaccuracy was the only way her reading was possible. When her toes were an inch away from the scale's edge, she held her breath and leaned over.

Zero. The skinny black dial couldn't have been more exact.

She was already up 5 pounds from her school physical the month before and now only 4 pounds from 190, and 14 pounds from the unthinkable 200. Two hundred! Had she really eaten *that* many Snickers in one month?

As her head began to spin and her knees tremble, she shoved the scale under her bed. She bent over, snatched her clothes from the floor, and tugged on her underwear and sweatpants. She shrugged one arm into her sweatshirt and frantically reached behind her for the other sleeve. She twisted and turned, unable to grab the material. She spun in a circle and craned her neck over her shoulder to see where exactly the sleeve was.

What she saw instead stopped her midspin.

Maggie hated mirrors. She avoided them at all costs, just as she did windows, clean appliances, shiny floors, and anything else in which she might catch her reflection. She hadn't really *seen* herself in months. But now she stood, completely paralyzed by her reflection in the dresser mirror.

There were the rolls around her middle, the anticipated

zigzagging of boob and belly stretch marks, and the way everything jiggled when she moved even the slightest bit. These were the typical overweight symptoms that could be found in any doctor's office or encyclopedia. But the worst part, the thing that made her heart drop to her knees, was her face.

Her flushed cheeks were like mini water balloons, ready to burst. Her dark eyes were squinty, as though the sun shone directly from the bedroom ceiling. And at last check, she'd had only one chin; now another half crept toward her neck.

If this was what people saw when they looked at her, then they had no idea who she was. She was an excellent student. A good daughter and sister. A loyal friend. (And she'd be the best girlfriend *ever* once Peter Applewood came around.) She loved books, movies, and talking on the phone. She wanted to go to college and find an enjoyable yet high-paying job. She wanted to get married, own a home, and have three happy, healthy children. She was a regular kid with regular-kid hopes and goals.

But she was still smart enough to know that no one her age looked at her and saw themselves.

She forced her arm into the other sweatshirt sleeve, jumped into bed, and reached for the Butterfingers under the mattress. When she grabbed a handful and flopped back, her head hit the pillow like it was made of wood and not feathers.

She dropped the candy and pulled the photo album out from under her pillow. She kept it there for when her mother realized its absence, but it remained unclaimed. She leaned against the wall and slowly flipped through the pages. When she came upon her school picture from the year before, she gently pulled it from its plastic slot and closed the album.

Just twelve months before, she'd looked like someone else—someone with actual cheekbones, dimples, and wide eyes. *What happened?*

She rested the picture against her nightstand lamp, brushed the Butterfingers from her bed, and pulled the covers over her head.

One hundred eighty-six unrecognizable pounds.

The truth was hard to swallow.

14.

"Water stick?"

Maggie stopped braiding the frayed strings on the knee of her jeans and sat up straight.

"They can hide it under peanut butter, cottage cheese, or a gallon of mint chocolate chip. It'll still just be water in disguise."

Maggie shifted in the metal folding chair, crossed one ankle over the other, and cleared her throat, careful not to distract the Pound Patrollers gathered in the middle of the room. By all counts, it was her turn to speak. She was still behind from last week, since they hadn't talked again after Arnie had joined the circle.

"Chocolate chip cookie dough." It was the first thing that came to mind. She closed her eyes and shook her head. Those unaware of her academic record would find it hard to believe.

She tried again.

"On the celery, I mean. That's what it would take, for me."

Arnie's eyes widened and he nodded in approval. "Good one."

Maggie forced her eyes to meet his. She tried to smile, but it was next to impossible as she fought the urge to crawl under her chair, run to the car, or hide behind one of the other Pound Patrollers. They might've been there for similar reasons, but even though she had no idea who he was, where he was from, or if she'd ever see him outside of the meetings, she was still uncomfortable that someone her age knew how she spent her Wednesday nights.

"Hey, I think we're onto something. Mothers across America want their kids to eat vegetables without whining, right? We could so market this! Instead of Ben and Jerry's and tie-dyed T-shirts, we could be Arnie and—"

"Maggie." At this rate, she could kiss her secret identity good-bye.

"Maggie." He smiled. "Arnie and Maggie, right, and we could wear, I don't know, togas or something."

She laughed. "Togas?"

"Piggy bank's depleted at the moment and togas we can make out of Mom's linen closet."

"What about ice cream fixings? And vegetables?"

"Believe me, our kitchen's stocked. We'll cut Mom in somehow, make her director of freezing or head mixer or something."

"Oh, Mag Pie!" Aunt Violetta sang across the room and waved. "There's a seat right here, next to me!"

Maggie sighed.

"Your mom?"

"Worse. Aunt. So I can't totally ignore her now and count on forgiveness later."

Maggie waved back and shook her head.

"It's not so bad up there. They're pretty funny, actually."

She shrugged. "Just not my thing."

"Mine either. Which is why I convinced my parents to let me come to this location, forty-five minutes away from my town and anyone I could possibly know."

"Maggie, sweetie, c'mon! How'll you know what I'm saying about you if you don't get over here?" Aunt Violetta winked.

"She's pretty cool, your aunt. Very nice." Arnie waved back as though he and Aunt Violetta were old friends.

"Yes, so nice that she's even volunteered to assist with the lookout of my *own good*."

"Ah, your own good." Arnie sighed and nodded. "Similar, I'm sure, to my *best interest*, which is supposedly what my mother has in mind."

He stood up, shook one leg and then the other until his cargo pants fell into place, tugged at the hem of his sweatshirt, and shoved his hands in his pockets.

"You joining the circle of truth this week?" he asked, peering down at her from underneath his red knit cap. "If you get bored, you can always help crack the mysterious case of the petty pizza thief," he offered, as though she might jump at the chance.

"The *what?*"

He leaned toward her and lowered his voice. "I *know* someone chows down next door before meetings. That circle's small and garlic's *potent!*"

"Okay, folks, let's get started, shall we?" Electra practically shouted over the excited din of Pound Patrollers.

"We'll swap notes, Sherlock!" Arnie called over his shoulder as he shuffled toward the circle, hands still deep in his sweatshirt pockets.

"So, who'd like to tell the group about this week's goal achievement?" Electra asked as everyone quieted and took to their metal folding chairs.

Samuel the Krispy Kreme addict waved his hand furiously.

"Yes, Samuel, thank you for starting us off," Electra said, taking her own seat and removing the pencil from behind her ear.

"Well," Samuel began, looking around at all the ladies to make sure he had everyone's attention, "as discussed last week, I had managed to eliminate one thousand five hundred extra calories a day by limiting my intake of those irresistibly scrumptious, fried, glazed, circular concoctions." Samuel licked his lips and winked at the woman sitting next to him.

As he paused and turned his eyes skyward for dramatic emphasis, the ladies nodded intently, seemingly captivated by the simple recap.

By the snack table in the back of the room, Maggie picked at her fingernails and pretended not to listen. She knew no one paid attention, but she rested her elbows on her knees and tilted her head toward the circle casually, just in case someone happened to notice her attempt to hear better.

"Well," he exhaled, "the plan was to kick off a new schedule of Krispy Kreme Mondays and Fridays, so that only two days out of the entire seven day week would involve the tremendous treats, making the other five days particularly trying to get through."

The women eagerly nodded and leaned in closer.

"But"—Samuel paused again, briefly closed his eyes— "there was a change of plans."

Maggie looked up as the room erupted in gasps, raised

eyebrows, and head shaking. Aunt Violetta even brought one hand up to her chest, as though the news was simply too much to bear.

Samuel held up his palms till the group once again grew silent.

"I have to admit, I didn't think I could do it. I thought about it and thought about it, struggled with my goal, and honestly just didn't think I was strong enough to give in to such temptation twice a week and not be tortured every other day. I feared falling off the bakery wagon!"

More head shaking and a handful of gasps. Maggie rolled her eyes. They were just donuts, for heavens' sake. What was the big deal? But she leaned even closer to the group, anyway.

"So yes, the plan changed. And *instead*"—he paused again, causing anxious titters throughout the room—"I went the *entire* week without *one* single bite of Krispy Kreme wonder!"

The group exploded in applause, hugs, and high fives, as though they all had something to do with his accomplishment.

"Another amazing week, Samuel. Whew!" Electra exclaimed, tapping on her clipboard to regain the group's attention. "You went above and beyond there, saving yourself another three thousand calories for the week! Marvelous, just marvelous!"

As Electra made notes, Samuel announced the following week's goal of cutting back on the chocolate chip pancakes he'd been eating to wean himself off the Krispy Kremes.

"Who's next? Arnold? Care to share?"

"No problemo." Arnie shifted in his seat. "Well, my goal for this week was to look for any problematic patterns in my eating habits by keeping a food diary."

"And how'd that go?" Electra asked. "Did you notice anything?"

"Did I *ever*!"

The group chuckled as Arnie whipped a folded packet of notebook paper from the side pocket of his cargo pants.

In the back of the room, Maggie practically fell out of her chair. He was going to actually share what he ate? What business was it of theirs? The only person who knew what she consumed on any given day was herself, and even she wasn't always certain.

"I took notes day and night, and don't think I've ever written so much in my entire life." Arnie held the wrinkled papers to his leg and smoothed them with one hand. "Okay!" He raised the papers in front of his face. "Day one. Breakfast with the parental units. Scrambled eggs, oatmeal, OJ. Lunch with Jackson and Drew. Turkey and mustard on whole wheat, low fat milk. Dinner with Rosalie—"

"*Rosalie?*" Samuel interrupted with a grin. "Might someone have a little girlfriend?"

Maggie silently thanked Samuel for his nosy teasing. If Arnie had a girlfriend, they had much less in common than she'd originally predicted.

"*No*, someone might have a little housekeeper." Arnie's cheeks turned pink as he cleared his throat again. "Dinner. Baked halibut, steamed asparagus, brown rice."

"That sounds wonderful," Aunt Violetta encouraged.

"Very healthy," the lady with the silver braid seconded.

"Doesn't it?" Arnie agreed. "Except that squeezed in the margins and above and under each meal"—he squinted and held the papers so close to his face that they touched his nose—"are the *snacks*. Walk to school: two blueberry muffins. Study hall vending machine break: potato chips and Pop-Tarts. Walk home: pint of pork fried rice and an egg roll." Arnie lowered the papers, looked to Electra, and sighed in defeat. "I think I need a bodyguard."

Electra smiled sympathetically. "It's a wonderful realization, Arnold." She made a note on her clipboard and addressed the rest of the group. "Invisible eating. Something we've all indulged in at one point or another. Arnie noticed that he eats normally throughout the day, even low-fat, nutritious foods for regular meals—regular meals eaten with other people, friends, family. But it's when he's alone that the problems start. Sweets and fattening treats he knows he really doesn't need that other people might disapprove of."

Maggie pictured the Snickers and Milky Ways waiting for her underneath her mattress, the same image she'd already indulged in three times since arriving at the meeting.

The group nodded knowingly, understandingly. They'd all been there.

"Great progress, Arnold," Electra praised. "Have you thought about what this week's goal might be, knowing now what you do about your habits?"

"To keep myself surrounded twenty four/seven?"

The group chuckled.

"No, seriously, I'll just be more aware. Take different routes to and from school, bring healthy snacks with me, so that next week my entire food log can fit on one piece of paper." Arnie refolded the packet of papers and shoved his hands back into his sweatshirt pockets.

"Fabulous place to start. Thank you for sharing. Good luck."

The meeting continued as each group member recounted the goal for the week, whether they'd met it, and what they planned to try for the following week. But Maggie stopped paying attention after Arnie's story. She thought instead of the bowl of cereal and banana she'd had for breakfast that morning, the grilled chicken salad with low-fat dressing she'd eaten at lunch, the turkey burger with a side of broccoli for dinner, and the scoop of chocolate frozen yogurt for dessert. Breakfast with her sister, lunch with Aimee, dinner with her family.

And then she thought of the Doritos she'd eaten after school, while watching *General Hospital* and before anyone else had come home. She'd eaten without thinking until her fingers glowed bright orange and her teeth were coated in a thin film of fake, powdery cheese, until her mother's Toyota had pulled in the driveway and Maggie had dashed to the kitchen, folding the top of the bag over only once so that it didn't appear as empty as it really was. She thought of the two chocolate cupcakes she'd hidden in her backpack "for later," as she'd put the Doritos back in the cupboard, and of her secret candy stash in her room. While the people who paid attention might have a clue as to what she was up to (her mom did do inventory for grocery shopping, after all), she made sure that no one ever actually *saw*.

Because if no one else saw, then maybe it didn't really happen? Was that what she thought?

After the last Pound Patroller update, Maggie waited through the concluding group song, hugs, air kisses, high fives, and the slow journey toward the apple slices and celery sticks. She moved away from the table but stayed nearby, pretending to be in search of something very important inside her purse (the contents of which consisted of her wallet, bubble gum, and strawberry lip balm), so that she didn't have to meet anyone's eyes or make conversation. She waited and rummaged until she was fairly certain all of the members had made it to the back of the room, and then she finally looked up.

Because while she wouldn't have any detective notes to swap, she was pretty sure she and Arnie could find lots to talk about.

She saw Aunt Violetta, Electra, Samuel, the woman with the silvery braid, and the rest of the members of varying shapes and sizes, holding their miniature cups of water and standing together, talking and laughing. They were all there, present and accounted for, except one.

Maggie looked quickly to the exit, saw the heavy glass door swinging slowly shut. She hurried over and peered through the darkened glass, and just barely saw the back of Arnie's head duck into a shiny silver SUV that sped away, as though its distance from Pound Patrollers couldn't widen quickly enough.

15.

Invisible eating. It sounded like some sort of carnival attraction or magic trick, and unfortunately it was one Maggie didn't need a magic wand to perform and one she wanted to forget.

She locked the bedroom door behind her and stood with her hands on her hips. Before she could change her mind, she rolled up her sleeves, took the purple garbage bin from beneath her desk, and squished down all of the empty Snickers and Milky Way wrappers that already overflowed onto the carpet. After making what she thought was enough room, she knelt by her bed and reached under her mattress with both hands.

She pulled out bag after bag of miniature Hershey bars, M&M's, Twizzlers, Swedish Fish, Andes Mints, Nerds, Tootsie Pops, Kit Kats, Twix, and Peppermint Patties, until her knees and back grew sore and she was up to her hips in creamy caramel, scrumptious sugar, and crunchy cookie filling. Up to her hips in millions of calories and thousands of fat grams. Up to her hips, which were three times the size of what they should be, because of all that surrounded her. The individual candy pieces looked like miniature Christmas gifts, wrapped in irresistible, shiny silver and gold wrappers. She found it no wonder that candy shelves were strategically placed by cash registers at the eye level of children. What little boy or girl could resist such pretty presents?

Maggie breathed through her mouth as she crammed the boxes and bags into the little garbage bin, avoiding the sweet scent that she fell asleep inhaling every night. She stuffed and smushed until nothing more would fit and six bags still lay scattered across the floor, which she briefly considered shoving back under the mattress to deal with later. She was tired, it was late, and she'd already made great progress.

But tonight there was no later. It had to be now or not at all.

Her heart thumping and perspiration beginning to shine on her forehead, Maggie opened and closed each of her desk drawers and rummaged through her closet, looking for some kind of disposable bag in which to dump the rest of the candy. She finally settled on an old duffel bag that she hadn't used in three years, shoved in the rest of the shiny evidence, and zipped up the bag in satisfaction. *Voilà.*

She pushed the garbage bin and bag against the wall by the door, took off her sweatshirt to cool down, and sat down at her desk with her notebook and calculator to do math homework.

She made it through the first page of problems in fifteen minutes. They were pretty easy, mainly a review of what they'd gone over in detail in class that day. She didn't know how some people preferred to just goof off throughout class, writing notes and whispering. How on earth did they manage?

Halfway through the second page of problems, she got stuck. She looked through her notes, read the textbook chapter that preceded the problems, and tapped her pencil on the desk until the point snapped. She sat for another fifteen minutes, trying to figure out the problem, until she grew bored and frustrated.

Boredom and frustration, it turned out, were two key components to the invisible eating magic trick.

Before she could stop herself, Maggie was out of her chair and standing above the bagged and binned candy. Not bothering to cover her nose or breathe through her mouth, she closed her eyes and inhaled the chocolate, peppermint, and licorice scents. It sure beat aromatherapy lotions or candles, both of which she'd attempted in hopes of relaxation and stress relief and which smelled more like the doctor's office in her opinion.

What would one little piece hurt? Just one little piece, to commemorate the occasion? A farewell, a parting gift to herself?

"Maggie, honey?" Her mother knocked on the door. "How was the meeting?"

She shook her head quickly, snapped herself out of the Hershey hypnosis. She cracked the door open just enough for her mother to see her but not her room.

"Fine." She tried to sound casual.

"Oh." Her mother blinked twice at Maggie's unexpected room block. "Can I come in?"

"Um." Maggie peeked quickly over her shoulder. Candy bars spilled out of the garbage bin and duffel bag right next to her feet. "Now's not really a good time."

"Homework?" She tilted her head sympathetically. "I know Thursdays are rough and these meetings really cut into—"

"It's okay." She waved one hand, grateful for the excuse. "I'm just trying to catch up."

Her mother winked. "Let me know if you need anything."

Maggie thanked her and closed the door, relieved.

This wasn't going to work. She needed to get the chocolate out of her room, out of her life, *now*. Otherwise what always happened would happen again. One piece of one kind of candy would lead to one piece of each kind of candy. One piece of each kind of candy would lead to two, three, four pieces. Soon she'd be stuffing bag after bag under her bed until she was back where she started. What she needed to do was get it out of the house and into the garbage barrels outside awaiting morning pickup.

Dropping to her knees one more time, Maggie peered under the mattress to make sure not one chocolate bar had gone unnoticed. If she didn't do it now, she'd do it some other time, when she actually hoped for something to have been left behind.

The floor was littered with forgotten socks and notebook paper, but clear of candy. Since she was there, she gathered a handful of socks. She was about to sit up when she noticed something else that had been hidden by her laundry. It was too far back to make out so she jumped up, yanked an empty hanger from the closet, and fell back to the ground.

Using the hanger as a plastic arm extension (if only hers were so thin!), Maggie lay flat on the ground and reached until she felt the hanger neck get a solid grasp on whatever she'd missed. She pulled it from underneath the bed slowly, shimmying backward until her butt smacked against the dresser.

When it was finally on the floor in front of her, Maggie sat back, crossed her legs, and brought it to her lap.

A box of tissues. She looked quickly to her nightstand where the same empty Kleenex box had sat for weeks.

This tissue box was inside a crocheted cover in the shape of a small white house, out of whose chimney sprouted pale blue tissues. Maggie had always loved the cover because each time one tissue was pulled, another popped up out of the chimney, as though an imaginary fire forever warmed the little home. It had been one of Aunt Violetta's first craft projects after her marriage, which she'd given to Maggie's mother. Its place was on her mother's nightstand, not underneath Maggie's bed.

And yet here it was, practically empty.

Maggie put the tissue box to the side and reached back under the bed with the hanger until the neck once again hooked onto something. She reached and pulled and reached and pulled until her arm and back grew sore. She reached and pulled, until she was up to her hips once again. Up to her hips, in a sea of crumpled, blue tissues.

Crumpled, blue tissues, which, when Maggie held them in her hands, were still damp.

16. The day after her bedroom candy cleansing, Maggie, Aimee, and Summer sat on her floor, surrounded by newspapers and magazines. It was the first time in months she didn't have to fear people in her room accidentally spotting the stray wrappers and bags she was always so careful to hide, which made focusing on their task much easier.

"Here's the *Maple Grove Sun*, the *Daily Dose*, and *People*."

Maggie raised her eyebrows.

"Brad Pitt and Angelina Jolie?" Aimee pointed to the magazine cover. "Brangelina? Adopting needy, non-American child number thirteen?"

"They're going to be in a new movie, too!"

Maggie laughed as Aimee held one finger to her mouth to keep Summer quiet.

"And I got *Today's News* and the *New York Times*," Maggie added, entering all the information onto the Master Multitasker. "So that's four newspapers, one motivational magazine—"

"And a phone book." Summer held up the yellow pages.

"Right." She finished typing, saved the document, and slid off the bed to the floor.

"So what exactly are we looking for?" Aimee sat next to Maggie and grabbed a newspaper.

"Anything outside. Landscaping, construction—".

"Dog walker?" Aimee suggested, opening the paper.

Summer scrunched her nose.

"Dad likes to *lead*, not be led," Maggie confirmed. "That's why no office jobs—not that he's in any position to be picky."

"Okay, outdoor, be-your-own-boss jobs. Got it."

"Also look out for full-time, competitive salary, and benefits," Maggie read from her spreadsheet. "Including health insurance, dental insurance, vacation time, and 401K. Those are the main things I've heard Mom talking about on the phone with Aunt Violetta."

"401 what?" Summer looked up from the *Maple Grove Sun*.

"Some retirement thing," Aimee explained. "You and

your company each put aside some money every month, and then you get it all when you retire or leave the company. So then when you're done working, you get money from the government *and* have all that extra money on top of your regular savings."

"How old *are* you?" Maggie teased.

"My parents are always talking about what money to use and which accounts to borrow from when they buy things. It's extremely boring, but I picked up some of it."

"Your parents must have a lot of money," Summer said in awe.

"Anyway." Maggie changed the subject when Aimee's cheeks turned pink. "We're looking for jobs that require physical labor."

"And that pay a million bucks," Summer added, turning back to the newspaper.

"So if you find anything good, just cut it out and I'll add it to the list," Maggie instructed, handing out scissors.

"Mags, you know I'm thrilled to help, but tell me again why your dad isn't doing this?"

Maggie shrugged. "I guess he doesn't realize how much he needs to."

They flipped pages, snipped ads, and made piles on the floor according to job type and pay. Using the phone book, they compiled the names and numbers of local landscape, construction, and pool companies. They worked until the room darkened from the setting sun and they heard the front door open and close.

"Mom's home!" Summer whispered, eyes wide. "I'll go distract her?"

"Good thinking!" Maggie winked. Their mother would never barge in, but Summer liked being included in such a top-secret project, and the more secretive it seemed, the more helpful she'd feel.

"So what's next?" Aimee asked, gathering the small piles scattered across the floor. "How are these going to go from tiny pieces of paper to actual jobs?"

Maggie sighed. "I haven't figured that out yet. I don't want Dad to feel pressured, because I know he's getting that from Mom. So I can't just give him these ads and the phone, but I also can't call places myself."

"Your voice *is* a little girly for Mr. Robert Bean."

"So." Maggie shrugged. "First thing's first. I'll enter the possibilities on the spreadsheet, sort them by type and salary, and go from there."

"What if you got help?"

Maggie looked up from her laptop. "I did. You and Summer."

"No!" Aimee patted Maggie's knee. "You could get someone to call and pretend to be your dad." She suggested this as though they hadn't just ruled out Maggie passing for a forty-six-year-old man.

"My pool of available bachelors is small, sorry." Maggie turned back to the laptop.

"What about Peter?"

Her mouth fell open.

"He seems so nice. I'm sure he'd help!"

"Yeah, okay. I'll be sure to bring it up the next time I stuff my books in his locker. What about you? This is such a great idea you must have other people in mind." Maggie was teasing, but Aimee did have a long list of admirers, each of whom would probably jump at the chance to win points.

"Please." Aimee rolled her eyes. "You know I can't be bothered."

Unlike Maggie, Aimee chose to remain crushless. She'd decided boys got in the way of friends and sports, and didn't want to deal with their silliness. Maggie envied her confident ability to choose. If Maggie ever swore off boys, it'd be because she gave in to the fact that they'd never look her way.

"Anyway," Aimee continued, "what's the big deal? What could it hurt? If he says no, oh well. But if he says yes, just think of all the time you could spend together. You do want your dad to have the best possible job, don't you?"

"Aim." Maggie closed the laptop. "You're my best friend, but you're also crazy. That would never work and I'm never going to ask. My family's money problems aren't going to get me anywhere with Peter."

"Fine." Aimee pouted.

"But I do appreciate your wanting to help two areas of my life at once."

"That reminds me." Aimee snapped her fingers. "There *is* one other area that could use improvement."

Maggie laughed. "There's more than that."

"But none as important as Water Wings," Aimee said, wiggling her eyebrows. "Tryouts are—"

"I changed my mind." Maggie winced. "I'm really sorry and don't worry, I'll still help you study. It's just not for me."

"But just last week at the pool you said—"

"I know, but I really don't have time. Now I have this job hunt on top of school and my activities. I just don't see how I'd squeeze it in."

Aimee frowned. "But are you totally sure? I could help you, we could do laps and practice the routines, and it would just be such a fun thing to do *together*. Think of all the possibilities! Meeting new people, swimming every day, going to other schools. Plus your mom would be totally thrilled."

Maggie sighed. If only joining the team was about fun and nothing more.

"I'm sorry, Aim. But I promise to be at all your meets!"

"Maggie, honey!" Her mother called through the bedroom door. "Mac and cheese in fifteen minutes!"

"Do you want to stay?" Maggie asked, scrambling to her feet when Aimee stood. "We can do homework and review notes for all our classes?"

"Sounds thrilling," Aimee teased. "But actually, I got a C yesterday on Madame DuMonde's quiz du jour, and Mom wants me home so she can see me physically open textbooks."

"You won't be on house arrest for long," Maggie assured. "And thanks for the help. I'm sorry again—"

Aimee threw her arms around Maggie's neck and squeezed. "Call me later."

After Aimee left, Maggie sank back to the floor and rested the laptop on her knees. She pulled up the Master Multitasker and inserted a new tab next to "Dad."

On the new "Water Wings" page, she added three tasks.

#1: Learn routines.

#2: Lose weight to avoid bathing suit trauma.

#3: Keep secret.

She highlighted #3, saved the document, and closed the laptop.

Because she really hadn't changed her mind. She'd still try out for Water Wings, but she'd decided to prepare on her own. Unlike Aimee, athlete extraordinaire, Maggie had to consider the risk of not making the team. She'd train day and night before tryouts, but the embarrassment she'd feel after training day and night and not making the team would be a million times worse if other people knew how hard she'd tried, only to fail. She felt like a big enough disappointment gaining the weight of a small child over the past year. She didn't want to disappoint anyone, especially her mother, ever again.

Of course she wouldn't stick one toe in the water if she wasn't fueled by that same disappointment and the desire to prove to everyone that she wasn't who they assumed she was. She wanted to show Anabel and Julia that she could do anything they could do, *and* in a silver two-piece. She wanted to show her parents that she could lose weight on her own, without the help of silly meetings. And she wanted to show her dad that the impossible really *was* possible.

As she was about to leave the room for dinner, she spotted her school photo from the year before resting on her nightstand. She picked it up and rubbed one finger over the dimples she hadn't seen in months.

She wanted to show herself, too.

The Melting of Maggie Bean

17. Two days after stuffing her entire candy stash in street-side garbage barrels, Maggie stood in the front of the drugstore, tightly clutching her plastic green change purse.

"Sweetie, get a load of this! SnackWell's now has zero fat, zero carbohydrate vanilla wafers!" The drugstore sales clerk smiled and held up a bright yellow box as he passed by with his cart. "Just got 'em in! Aisle two!" He winked.

"No, thanks." She smiled quickly, her cheeks instantly warm, before hurrying as far away from aisle two as she could get.

She'd only spent time in aisle three, the candy aisle, so she had to peek down the rest in pursuit of her new weekly survival kit. She dashed past pet supplies, makeup, medicine, shampoo, and toilet paper and didn't stop until the very last aisle.

Aisle ten. Pens, notebooks, computer paper, and, at the very end, magazines.

Without even looking at their contents, Maggie picked up as many shiny, boldly colored magazines as her arms would hold: *Glamour*, *Cosmopolitan*, *Vogue*, *Mademoiselle*, *YM*, *Seventeen*, and *Lucky*, those she'd seen other girls reading on the bus or in study hall. She tried not to fixate on the cover models, their blemish-free skin, snow-white teeth, pencil-thin legs, and flat tummies. The intimidating perfection was exactly what she'd fixate on later, after she'd paid for the magazines, brought them home, and read them cover to cover. If she looked too closely now, before she'd forked over her allowance savings, she just might give up entirely and take an unintended trip back to aisle three.

"Need a hand?"

This sales clerk really paid far too much attention to her.

"No, thanks." She shook her head without looking up. Spotting one last magazine to add to her pile, she leaned forward so that the stack was held in place between her torso and the magazine rack and carefully reached toward the bottom shelf.

"Sure about that?" he asked as the magazines slid from their holding spot and fell all over the floor.

Maggie knelt down and gathered her self-help guides. She hoped there was an article among them about how to curb her clumsiness.

The sales clerk crouched down to help before she could refuse. As he handed her copies of *Vogue* and *InStyle*, she noticed he wore a Swiss Army watch with a black leather band and silver face, just like—

"Peter?" She froze and felt the familiar heat rise to her cheeks.

"Doing a research project on modern beauty rituals?" he asked with a smile.

"Sorta." She focused on keeping her hands steady so that she didn't drop again all the magazines she'd just picked up.

"That's PhD-worthy, if you ask me."

"What're you doing here?" She gathered the remaining issues, brought them to her chest, and stood up.

"My own research."

"*Sports Illustrated* and *National Geographic*?"

He shrugged. "Athletes and polar bears are more alike than you'd think."

She laughed. "I'll be sure to pick up your thesis from the library."

"So"—he motioned to her stack—"can I help you to the register?"

She quickly shook her head. The idea of walking with Peter down any kind of aisle was enough to send instant goosebumps up and down her arms, but she didn't want him to get any closer looks at her research material. She'd picked up *Shape* for its foldout "bun and tummy" exercises, and she didn't need him to read about it on the magazine's cover.

36 dates, 24 phone calls, 36 kisses.

"No, I think I've got it." She smiled and held the stack tighter against her chest.

He nodded. "Right, okay. Well, good luck—with your project, I mean."

Did he look disappointed? Was she imagining things?

"You too."

As he walked away, she shook her head and tried to regain focus. Now was not the time to get silly and girly because of Peter Applewood. If all went well, there'd be plenty of time for that later.

Her arms heavy, she hobbled down the aisle and balanced the stack of magazines on one leg as she grabbed a roll of Scotch tape and a pair of scissors. She dropped everything on the counter by the register and then ran to aisle nine: hair products, lotions, soap, and makeup. She found the same pink mascara tube that Anabel and Julia had carried when Maggie was last there, and added lipstick, nail polish, and tweezers to her growing pile.

The cashier tapped a bandaged fingertip on the counter.

"That all?" she asked, sounding bored.

Maggie quickly ran through the list in her head and nodded.

The woman scanned the gum and added it to the third plastic bag.

"Forty-seven dollars and fifty-two cents."

Maggie's mouth dropped open as she looked at the glowing green numbers on the register and then down at her purchases on the counter. This new project was certainly more expensive than maintaining her secret candy stash, and would wipe out her entire allowance savings. She considered putting some of the magazines back, but quickly decided against it. It was a small price to pay for the benefits she hoped to derive, and Maggie knew she'd wonder later if whichever magazine she returned held the one secret or beauty tip that would put her back on the social radar. Three nintey-nine wasn't worth the risk.

She took her time counting out the exact change and enjoyed the fact that she didn't have to hurry out of embarrassment the way she usually did when leaving the store with bags and bags of chocolate. She even let herself lean one arm on the counter and wait for a receipt, as though every purchase was so casual.

Maggie carefully guided the scissors around the Gap model's pronounced, blushed cheekbones, slender neck, delicate shoulders, perfect chest, and tiny waist, where she stopped in brief, wistful admiration. She tightened her grip and continued down the model's hips, legs, and narrow ankles until the entire figure popped from the magazine page like a paper doll. She held the cutout gently, as though one wrong move might rip the model—and Maggie's grand plan—into a zillion pieces.

She gently attached two pieces of Scotch tape to the model's back before sliding off the bed, stepping over the wobbly stack of shredded magazines, and surveying her room.

A Victoria's Secret brunette winked in leopard-printed lingerie from her underwear drawer. A green-turtle-necked, freckled J.Crew blonde grinned from the top of her jewelry box. And a cargo-panted Abercrombie & Fitch redhead peeked from the top of her nightstand. These girls modeled the clothes that everyone could wear but her, and the reminders were plastered from floor to ceiling.

Spotting an empty patch on her closet of JCPenney plus-size, elastic-waist pants and stretchy sweaters, Maggie patted the Gap model into place.

Satisfied with her new bedroom decor, Maggie flopped back onto the bed and retrieved the stack of articles from her nightstand. Low-fat, high-fat, low-carb, sugar-free, cabbage soup, bananas, juice fasts, protein shakes, meat only, veggies only. There were a thousand different diets, and it could take a thousand years to figure out which one worked for her.

But Water Wings tryouts were less than three weeks away. She didn't have the kind of time a normal, balanced diet required. She needed to show Anabel, Julia, her dad, and everyone else. She needed to lose a lot of weight, and she needed to lose it *fast*.

She pulled her laptop to the bed, loaded the Master Multitasker, and clicked on "Water Wings."

Underneath the first three tasks she'd added three more.

#4: Buy magazines for diet/exercise tips.

#5: Plaster room with motivational models.

#6: Get sweating!

She proudly checked off #4 and #5, pushed the laptop aside, and grabbed the bun and tummy foldout from the stack of articles.

After making sure her door was locked, Maggie slid off the bed and spread the exercise guide across the floor.

She lay on her back, raised her legs in the air, and tried to lift her head and shoulders toward her knees. Her stomach jiggled, her neck strained, and she held her breath in concentration. When she thought her head might snap off, she dropped her shoulders back to the floor.

Only three more crunches to go and she could check off #6.

18.

"Remember when we'd go to the movies?" Summer asked without looking up from *Today's News*.

"For Friday night openings and not Sunday afternoon matinees." Maggie nodded.

"And we'd get real popcorn and soda from the snack bar—"

"Instead of smuggling snack bags and cans from home." Maggie turned the last page of the *Maple Grove Sun* and tossed it to the floor. "Yup."

"I hate the way people turn around when we open the cans." Summer pouted. "Like we're doing something wrong."

"How about Monday Mania? With party hats, balloons, board games, and takeout to celebrate the beginning of another week?"

Summer laid the paper in her lap. "Now Mondays are just like every other day."

Maggie rolled onto her stomach and rested her chin on her folded arms. "What I think I miss most of all is Mom and Dad just getting along."

Summer's eyes widened. "The fighting's the worst."

"It's like they barely know each other."

"But I miss all of us," Summer added. "The way we'd all hang out."

"*We* still hang out," Maggie said brightly.

"It's not the same." Summer looked down and fiddled with the newspaper.

Maggie sat up and slid off the bed. "What do you mean?"

Summer shrugged. "After Dad stopped working and they started arguing, you began hiding in your room."

"I didn't—"

"It's okay." Summer glanced up. "I understand. But when you disappear after dinner, Dad watches TV and Mom cleans or talks on the phone. I don't know." She bit her lip. "I just get sad."

Maggie scooted closer and put one arm around Summer's shoulders. "We're all still here. And don't you worry." She patted the newspaper. "We're going to fix things."

Summer nodded. "I know."

"And then we'll have Monday Mania every day of the week."

Summer grinned.

"So." Maggie squeezed her tightly and then straightened the small piles scattered across the floor. "These are all from today's papers?"

"Yup." Summer sat up straighter. "Sorted by type and money."

"Perfect." She carefully gathered the clippings. "I'll enter them on the list, and we're done for the day."

"Do you need me for anything else?" Summer asked hopefully.

Maggie shook her head. "Your job here is done."

"Does that mean I have to do my homework?"

"You can do whatever you want." Maggie laughed. "But that's what I'm going to do."

"Okay." Summer sighed and stood up. "But I'm right down the hall if you need me!"

Maggie closed the door after her sister and quietly turned the lock. She sat on the floor, opened her laptop, and loaded the Master Multitasker. She'd already finished her homework and Dad's job could wait, so the cursor flew by every tab but the last.

She clicked on "Water Wings" and examined the growing list.

#7: No bread, pasta, ice cream, cake, candy, or anything yummy.

#8: No hamburgers, hot dogs, pizza, or anything fried.

#9: No whole milk, fruit juices, or regular soda.

#10: 100 crunches, 100 lunges, and 50 pushups, twice a day, every day.

#11: Befriend the scale.

#12: Memorize routine tapes!

She'd pored over her entire magazine stash the night before and noted the most important or frequently suggested tips. The biggest trend seemed to be eating foods high in protein and low in carbohydrates, which meant she'd live on chicken and lettuce until tryouts. Even fruits and vegetables were bad for dieting because they contained natural sugar.

She checked off numbers seven through nine in that day's column. She'd had cottage cheese for breakfast and a grilled chicken salad with no dressing for lunch, and water instead of soda. She smiled at her logged accomplishments. It wasn't easy, especially when she had to stop the school cafeteria lady from plopping chicken nuggets and onion rings onto her tray. Or when her mother made an entire pan of Rice Krispies Treats for Summer's lunchbox. Or when she was in her room after dinner, thinking nonstop about peanut M&M's. But the sacrifices were worth the pride she felt when logging her accomplishments every night, and that's what she reminded herself with every craving.

She saved the spreadsheet changes and pushed the laptop aside.

She tackled the second half of #10 next, alternating twenty crunches with twenty lunges and ten pushups, five times. She had to stop after the third cycle to let her muscles rest, so she quickly entered the latest job ads into the Master Multitasker before resuming her crunches.

She hoped she was doing them right. Her abs hurt, but when she looked down as she lifted up, all she saw was mush. Her muscles were so hidden, she could only hope they were still there and working.

After finishing the last of the lunges and pushups, Maggie sat up and checked off #10. When she saw what was next, she quickly pulled the scale out from under her bed, tugged off her shorts, and kicked off her sneakers. If she didn't just take a deep breath and get it over with, it'd never get done.

She wiggled her toes and waited for the black dial to stop moving.

It's just temporary. Whatever number it lands on will be lower soon.

Inhaling deeply, she peeked over her stomach.

182.

She gasped, backed off the scale, checked the initial setting, and stepped on again.

182.

She'd thrown out her candy stash only five days before and she'd already lost four pounds. That was practically a pound a day!

She smiled at the unexpected number. No one but her would be as happy to weigh so much, but it was *progress*. That meant if she kept eating the way she was and exercised twice as much, she could lose nearly twenty pounds before tryouts! All the magazines said she should expect to lose about five pounds the first week and one or two every week after that, but maybe her body worked differently. Maybe she'd lose weight faster because her body needed to drastically adjust to its chocolate withdrawal.

She jumped off the scale, pulled on her shorts and sneakers, and happily typed her new weight into the Master Multitasker. Both the "Dad" and "Water Wings" spreadsheets were covered in green checkmarks. There was only one task she hadn't completed, and that was a work in progress.

She jumped up and turned on the small television on top of her dresser. The routine tape she'd borrowed from Ms. Pinkerton was still in the VCR, so she pushed Play and lay on the floor.

As she circled her arms and lifted her legs, she felt her hidden muscles tightening and contracting. The carpet wasn't as cool or refreshing as pool water, but when Anabel and Julia smiled in the video, she had no problem smiling back.

19.

"Maggie, are you okay?" Aimee whispered, plopping a stack of spiral notebooks onto the library table and sitting down.

Maggie's eyes fluttered open. Why was Aimee looking at her like that?

"What's wrong?" Maggie asked.

Aimee raised her eyebrows. "You were just sleeping sitting up. Your head was about to drop onto the dictionary. I know from personal experience that's no way to build your vocabulary."

Maggie shut her eyes tightly, opened them again, and registered the book in front of her.

"Mr. Webster may have been smart, but he certainly wasn't very exciting." She attempted to laugh, but a yawn got in the way.

"Seriously, what's up? What planet are you on?" Aimee looked away and unloaded textbooks from her backpack.

Maggie sat up straighter and shook her head to wake up her drowsy brain.

"Nothing's up. I'm here. Everything's great."

"Yeah, which is why you've been late to first period the past three days. And why you weren't at Mathletes on Monday or French Club yesterday."

Maggie furrowed her eyebrows. Tried as she had to get her to join, Aimee wasn't in Mathletes or French Club. "How did you—"

"Mr. Coogan and Madame DuMonde both asked me about you in class. Under normal circumstances, I would've known exactly what to tell them."

"Oh."

Aimee looked at her expectantly.

Maggie waved her hand. "I haven't been anywhere. I've just had to get home right after school this week. No biggie." She picked up a pencil and tapped its eraser against the dictionary, distracted.

Aimee raised her eyebrows.

"I've just had stuff to do," Maggie said quickly. "Stuff around the house. And outside the house. But everything's fine, really."

Aimee frowned but returned her attention to her backpack. Maggie knew she was trying to give her another chance to talk about what was really up without asking further questions.

"So, how are you? How's training going?"

As she rummaged through her backpack, Aimee shot her a look. "Shaved off three more seconds, and am up to two hundred sit-ups a night," she reported, reluctantly accepting Maggie's subject change. "And Justine Jackson offered to help me with another routine, so that's good."

Maggie nodded. Justine was a Water Wing whose circle of friends actually extended beyond the circle of bodies in the pool.

"Do you think you'd want to come by the pool after school today? She's going to run through the routine with me, but I'd love to get your totally honest opinion on how ridiculous I really look."

"You won't look ridiculous. You couldn't."

"I'm sure I'll look like a drunken crab. But I'm okay with that." Aimee grinned. Victoriously pulling a bag of trail mix from her backpack, she looked at Maggie. "It'd be nice to hang out. I feel like we haven't really talked in days."

It had been days. And the last time was over a marathon math study session, during which Maggie forced Aimee to discuss numbers only.

"I know, Aim, but not today. Soon though, I promise."

Maggie tried to listen as Aimee talked about her big afternoon English test—they were in the library to study, after all—but she was very distracted by the open bag of trail mix sitting on the table between them. Every time Aimee took a handful she turned the bag back toward Maggie. It was an open invitation to help herself. She'd only had a salad all day, and her stomach had been growling for an hour. And the trail mix was her favorite kind, with peanuts, raisins, and imitation M&M's.

As they opened their textbooks, Peter Applewood entered the library, laughing with his friends and assorted Water Wings members. She turned her head before he caught her watching, and instantly dismissed all trail mix thoughts.

The scale had read 181 that morning. She knew what she was doing.

20. "Who's hungry?"

"Daddy?"

"It's me, Summer sunshine!"

Maggie muted the television when she noticed his pressed khakis, blue button-down shirt, and tie. She couldn't remember the last time she'd seen him in anything other than jeans and flannel shirts.

"What's going on?" Her mother stood in the kitchen doorway, knife in one hand, carrot in the other. She looked him up and down, eyebrows raised.

"Honey," Maggie's father rubbed his palms together. "We're going out to dinner."

"What? Why? I've already started the chicken," her mother protested.

He waved his hand. "Tomorrow, we microwave. Tonight, we let someone else cook!"

Maggie looked back and forth between her parents. Her mother was clearly confused. Not only did they never go out to eat, but she'd probably used coupons to help buy the carrot she still held, and had to wonder how they'd pay for a meal prepared and served by other people.

"But," her mother protested, "it's nobody's birthday, our anniversary was months ago, and we can't afford it." She whispered the last part.

Her father shook his head and smiled. "Don't worry about a thing. It's all taken care of."

As her mother lowered the carrot in wonder, Maggie gasped, switched off the television, dropped the remote to the coffee table, and dashed down the hallway toward her bedroom.

"I'll be ready in five minutes!" she called over her shoulder.

Because if her suspicions were right, if her father really had gotten a new job, she'd blow up balloons herself to celebrate the return to normalcy.

"This place is so *fancy*," Summer whispered excitedly.

"Dad must have *very* good news," Maggie whispered

back, unfolding the white cloth napkin and laying it in the lap of an old denim skirt, the only one that still fit.

Very good news was an understatement, because when she'd expected him to turn into Friday's or Applebee's, their usual restaurant stops, her father had kept driving until reaching Nora's, the most expensive restaurant in town. They'd passed by the converted Victorian house numerous times over the years, had commented on the candles in the windows and the white Christmas lights in the trees, but had never actually parked the car and gone inside.

And now Maggie understood why.

In addition to those in the windows, countless candles made the room glow so that overhead, electrical lighting was unnecessary. The tables were draped in soft white linen and wildflower arrangements, the chairs were covered in creamy velvet, and long, sheer curtains flowed from the ceiling to the floor. Vinyl booths and free refills were suddenly things of the past.

"Water is fine," her mother said quietly when the waitress asked for drink orders.

"Nonsense!" her father protested loudly. "We'll have a bottle of your best merlot and Shirley Temples for the girls."

"Wow!" Summer mouthed to Maggie, eyes wide. They

only had Shirley Temples at wedding receptions or other free, fancy occasions.

Maggie watched her mother's fingers tighten around the leather-bound menu.

"And girls, order anything you want, anything at all." He winked before ducking his head behind the menu.

Maggie's mouth watered at the entrée choices: capellini pomodoro, fettucine Alfredo, penne a la vodka. When she could feel the warm noodles in her belly, she shook her head and forced her eyes to the pasta-free, chicken and fish sections. She didn't care if her father had been elected mayor; the scale had read 179 that morning and no occasion was worth regaining a single pound.

"So." Her father clapped his hands together after they'd ordered. "I have news."

Her mother reached for her wine glass. Maggie sat up straight and grinned at Summer.

"Now, nothing's definite, so let's not get too excited, but I have a potential job opportunity."

Her mother's mouth fell open and she lowered the wine glass slightly.

"An *opportunity*?"

Her father cleared his throat at her mother's disappointment.

"Yes, but it's just about a done deal."

"But opportunities are great!" Maggie exclaimed. "They lead to other things!"

Her mother forced a smile. "Well, where? Doing what?"

Her father waved his hand. "Details, details. They're not worth getting into right now. But suffice it to say that if it all works out, we'll be all right." He sipped his wine. "We'll be *better* than all right."

"Can't you tell us anything about it? Is it a company? Is it local?" Her mother's voice was cautious.

He shook his head. "I'll tell you everything when it's finalized."

Her mother sat back in her chair, frowning slightly. "Will that be soon?"

He awkwardly patted her hand that lay on the table between them. It was the grandest affectionate gesture Maggie had witnessed between them in months.

"It'll work out. Don't worry."

Maggie fiddled with the cherry in her drink as her mother poured herself another glass of wine.

"So, sunshine! Filet mignon. Good choice!"

Her mother let him change the subject and they talked about random things before and during dinner: the weather, the new shopping complex just south of the highway, movies—nothing especially important, but still meaningful because they actually talked, *together*. Maggie relaxed in a way she never could during meals at home, and she knew her mother did the same, with some help from the wine.

"Well, that was extraordinary," he declared when they finished, patting his belly and handing the waitress a credit card.

"Hey, Maggie."

Her head snapped up and she quickly made sure the cloth napkin in her lap adequately covered her belly before turning around.

"Peter, hi!" She brought both palms to her pink cheeks. "Are you here with your family?" She peeked behind him.

"We come every week. It's my mom's favorite place."

"My dad got a great new job!" she exclaimed before she could dwell on the fact that his family could afford to eat things like *salmon oreganato* four times a month.

"Cool, congrats." He nodded and smiled at her father.

Maggie twisted in her chair to better make conversation.

"I'm sorry, sir," the waitress said quietly.

Maggie's breath caught.

"This credit card came back declined." Her voice was apologetic, as though she was embarrassed for them. "Might you have another?"

Her father's eyes widened briefly before he reached for his wallet.

"So! English!" she declared, hoping the volume of her voice was suitably distracting. "Did you finish *Macbeth*?"

Peter smiled slightly. "I should get back to my family. I'll see you in school."

She sighed, turned back to the table, slumped in the velvet chair, and watched as her father's fingers trembled through the pockets of his wallet. Closed her eyes as her mother shook her head and pulled a thin envelope of cash from her purse. Maggie had been grocery shopping with her mother enough to know that she handed the waitress a large portion of her carefully budgeted monthly allowance, and that they'd probably live on canned tuna and baked beans until her next payday.

"No worries!" Her father's voice was unnaturally bright as the waitress walked away with cash and he drained his wine glass. He placed the empty glass on the table, wiped his mouth with one hand, and looked down at his lap. "No worries."

21. With just two weeks remaining before tryouts, Pound Patrollers was the last place Maggie wanted to be. She was doing just fine losing weight on her own and needed every free minute to memorize the routine tapes. She'd even considered faking sudden illness, but then remembered one reason the meeting might not be a total waste.

"Waffle cone crowns." Arnie flopped in the chair next to hers.

"Okay…" She sat up straighter in her chair.

"To go with the togas, instead of cheesy gold wreaths," he explained.

She nodded, pretending to seriously consider the proposition.

"Just picture it." He spread his hands in the air as though

the imaginary creation floated before them. "Red, blue, green, purple, any color of the rainbow, and topped with broccoli florets instead of sugar sprinkles."

Maggie laughed at the excitement in his voice.

"And!" He slapped his knee. "The best part: customer customization. Kids can decorate however they want. Brussels sprouts, green beans, cauliflower." He leaned back in the chair and crossed his arms over his chest in satisfaction. "They'll be all the rage once our parlor/gift shop combos sweep the nation."

"This is quite the vision."

"Yoo-hoo, Mag Pie!" Aunt Violetta half stood from her chair in the group's circle. "Two seats, right here! One for you, one for Arnold!" She smiled wide and flashed two thumbs up.

"Did she really just do that?" Arnie asked without moving his lips as he smiled and waved.

Maggie wagged her finger back and forth until Aunt Violetta playfully pouted and sat back down.

"You're dressed down tonight." Maggie pointed to his blue sweatpants.

"For the gym. My mom's latest and greatest. So I can be *as good as new*, as soon as possible."

"At least she didn't think spandex would get you better faster."

"Silver linings, always appreciated."

"Is the gym around here?"

He shook his head. "Working out is apparently way cooler than these meetings. There was no room for geographical negotiation. But it's not so bad—a little cardio here, a little weight training there. There's even a pool, though I never go in."

"A pool, huh?" Maggie almost looked up to see if a cartoon lightbulb glowed above her head. Endless analysis of Water Wings routine tapes was helpful, but there was only so much she could master on her bedroom carpet. And while it might seem essential, she hadn't yet convinced herself that practicing (and embarrassing herself) in front of other people in the school pool was a requirement to making the team. She'd settled for hoping that her body would just sense the graceful moves when the time came.

"It's small, just two lanes, so there's usually a wait, which I don't have the patience for. I do the necessary time and get out."

"Oh." She bit her lip and the cartoon lightbulb dimmed. She felt him look at her.

"What's up? Itching for a dip?"

She hadn't told anyone about her plan because she hadn't wanted to set anyone (besides herself) up for potential disappointment. But she so wanted to tell *someone*, and Arnie was as safe a bet as she was going to get. He hadn't known her long enough to form any expectations or permanent opinions, and they didn't even go to the same school, so there was no way anyone else would find out.

She glanced toward the circle of gathering Pound Patrollers. If she kept her mouth closed, she'd miss her chance. She took a deep breath, turned toward Arnie, and met the green eyes watching her from underneath his red knit cap.

"Actually, yes."

"Are you for real?" Maggie asked, joining Arnie at the end of the dock.

"You wanted a place to practice."

"Yes, but when you mentioned plan B after not being able to sneak me into your gym pool fee-free, a *lake* wasn't what I had in mind."

"Hey, synchronized swimming is a tough sport. If you can't hack it—"

"I'm tough! It's just, like, October." Maggie breathed into her cupped hands and tucked them in her armpits.

"Which makes this," Arnie declared with a sweep of one arm, "all yours." He poked her shoulder.

Maggie peered over the dock's edge. "Are there creatures?"

"Yes, water snakes. Big ones. Think *Anaconda*."

Maggie's mouth fell open.

He rolled his eyes. "Mud Puddle Lake is manmade! The scariest things in there are floating scraps of busted inner tubes or abandoned flip-flops."

Maggie looked over her shoulder at the two-story luxury log cabin behind them. "I can't believe that's your *summer* house."

He shrugged. "Workaholic parents. It's a perk, I guess."

"You *guess*? I can't even imagine the fun you must have here."

"Yeah, Mom's a thrill with her waterproof laptop, and Dad's a hoot with iced tea in one hand and cell phone in the other."

A deck wrapped around the entire rear of the house, and, despite summer's end, a hammock still hung between two trees. Two Adirondack chairs faced the water. Maggie tried to picture anyone sitting in one of those chairs and typing away at a keyboard. If she ever had the chance to spend any amount of time at such a place, work would certainly be the last thing on her mind.

She shook her head.

"They can't be that bad. You *are* named after the Terminator."

"It was more for his Mr. Universe title, actually. Mom had high hopes."

Arnie picked up a rock, threw it halfway across the lake and lowered himself to the dock, dangling his legs over the side.

"Well, at least they both *have* jobs."

"Not everyone has to work."

"True." She lowered herself next to him. "But my dad hasn't in a long time. And we don't have a buffer like this." Maggie gestured to the vacant vacation homes dotting the circumference of the lake. "We don't even own *one* home."

He shrugged. "They're just wood and nails."

She'd take wood and nails over a pile of splinters, any day.

"At least your dad's around, right? I hardly ever see mine."

She nodded. "He's definitely around. It'd probably be helpful if he was around *less*, actually."

"He gets in the way?" Arnie asked, as though this was something he heard could happen to other kids.

"No," she shrugged. "He just focuses on the wrong things, I think."

"ESPN and chicken wings?" He nodded in understanding.

"More like Jeopardy and Pound Patrollers. My going was his big idea."

Arnie looked down at the water, giving her time to elaborate.

Tricia Rayburn

"Is today a gym day?" she asked before he could respond, poking his blue sweatpants.

"Just like every day," he said, accepting her subject change. "But it'll be one quick session on the Precor Elliptical Trainer, because I have band rehearsal tonight."

"You're in a band?"

"I'd hoped Precor Elliptical Trainer would've been suitably distracting."

She dismissed the notion with a wave of her hand. "Old news. Like running, but without the pressure on your knees, according to *Cosmo*."

"*Cosmo*? Ew."

She rolled her eyes. "Marching or rock?"

He raised his eyebrows at her.

"Okay, what instrument?"

He fiddled with the stones scattered across the dock before settling on one, reaching his arm back and flinging it halfway across the lake.

"The flute!" He smacked one hand to his forehead. "The little girly flute."

She grinned. "Any good?"

"Five years of private lessons have taught me something, yes."

"Well, that should make your parents happy, right?"

He hurled another rock across the water. "Right. And it just might, if they ever heard me play." He jumped up, shook out his sweatpants, stuffed his hands into the pockets of his sweatshirt, and looked at her from underneath his red knit cap. "Anyway, I have to head out. But feel free to stay as long as you want."

She looked up at him, squinting against the afternoon sun. "No quick dip before you go?" She knew she needed privacy to practice, but she was still disappointed that he was leaving so soon.

He laughed as he headed back down the dock.

"It's *October*," he called over his shoulder. "That water's ice cold. You gotta be crazy!"

She picked up a rock and playfully tossed it after him. She waited until he climbed the back stairs and disappeared into the house before standing up, shedding her sweats, and facing the lake.

Goosebumps sprang instantly and her knees shook. It was now or never, and with tryouts less than a week away, there was no room for the latter. So she squeezed her nose, closed her eyes, and, before she could crawl back into the safety of her sweats or think about the warmth of her bedroom comforter, jumped.

22.

"Maggie, honey," her mother called through the bedroom door. "Aimee's on the phone!"

Maggie stopped jogging in place, wiped her forehead with one arm, and took three deep breaths before attempting to respond.

"Can I call her back?"

She heard her mother speak into the portable phone.

"She said yes, as long as you really do this time!"

Maggie stood in the middle of the room with her hands on her hips. Her chest swelled and dropped and her heart drummed in her ears so loudly that she barely heard her mother's soft footsteps retreat back down the hallway. Once certain no one stood directly outside her door, she waited an extra thirty seconds before turning the television back on, and another thirty before pressing Play on the VCR.

Because if she looked anything like the curly-haired little man in extra-short striped shorts springing across the thirteen-inch screen, she'd be defenseless against the inevitable teasing.

She had the fifty-minute aerobics routine memorized now. Five minutes of stretching, ten minutes of warm-ups, twenty minutes of low-impact aerobics, ten minutes of floor work, and five minutes of cool down. She'd found the ancient exercise tape tucked between *Gone with the Wind* and *Breakfast at Tiffany's*, two of her mother's favorites. After her very first attempt, her stomach muscles hurt more from laughing at the feather-haired women in pastel leotards and matching leg warmers than from the two-minute sit-up session. But by the second day she'd learned Richard Simmons sweats to the oldies for good reason: The cheesy music served as a hilarious distraction from the weird positions and bodily contortions that worked muscles she'd never known.

She was dripping her way through a third set of high kicks when a knock on the door made her stumble backward and drop onto the bed.

"Dinner's ready!" Summer announced, throwing open the door before Maggie could get her footing.

She jumped up and, suddenly aware that she wore only shorts and a sports bra and that her stomach probably glistened in the glow of the television screen, grabbed a pillow.

"Whatcha doing?" Summer peeked around the door. "Can I try?"

"I'll meet you at the table, okay?" Maggie tried to sound calm as she clutched the pillow to her stomach.

"But it looks like fun," Summer said hopefully.

Maggie sighed and flopped on the bed. "Go ahead." She would've pushed anyone else back out the door.

Despite her annoyance, Maggie couldn't help but envy the way Summer jogged in place and waved her arms over her head. Richard Simmons said that if she could hold a conversation while exercising, she was working at a good pace, and while there was never anyone to converse with, she practiced by answering Richard whenever he asked a question. If he asked if she felt the burn, the best she could muster was "uh-huh," even though she thought, *Yes, like a midsummer lightning storm!*

Her sister could've talked about the burn, how she didn't feel it, and the contents of her Texan pen pal's latest letter.

As her sister bounced around the room, Maggie halfheartedly reached for her laptop. She clicked on the Master Multitasker and the "Water Wings" tab.

177.

She sighed. It hadn't been updated in two days. Despite hardly eating and doubling her workouts, she hadn't lost a single pound since.

Summer came to an abrupt stop and flopped next to Maggie. "That *is* fun. Is it for school? A gym project or something?" She spoke clearly, her breathing normal.

Maggie tried to smile. "Or something." Her heart still throbbed in her chest and perspiration rolled down her cheeks.

"Okay, well, Mom said five minutes till dinner."

Maggie waited until the door clicked shut before standing and tossing the pillow back on the bed. Were nine lost pounds really not that noticeable? She knew not to expect great observational skills from a ten-year-old, but did Summer really think she sweat like a pig for *fun*?

"Sweetie, Aimee's on the phone again," her mother called. "She said it's important."

Maggie cracked the door just enough to take the phone from her mother.

"I said I'd call you back." She didn't *mean* to sound so huffy. It wasn't Aimee's fault she hadn't lost another pound. But weren't best friends supposed to have magical mood sensors that detected, among other things, the difference between good and bad talk times?

"Sorry, I know you can't really talk—"

Tricia Rayburn

Oh.

"—but I couldn't wait and you haven't been so quick to call me back lately."

Ignoring the phone neglect jab (mostly because it was true), Maggie sat on the bed. "No problem. What's up?"

"Well, after volleyball today a few girls and I went to Krispy Kreme."

"Uh-huh," Maggie said patiently. Aimee didn't know about Pound Patrollers or Maggie's diet. She didn't know not to inspire thoughts of frosted donuts.

"And when we walk in, Julia Swanson's sitting at a table by herself. By the time we get our food and sit down, she's still alone. As in, Anabel's missing."

"Missing?"

"Well, not there. You know bathroom breaks don't even split those two. Anyway, I'm getting very curious when in walks Peter."

Maggie was just about to reach for her laptop when her stomach lurched. "Peter Applewood?"

"So, I'm waiting for the rest of the baseball team to follow," Aimee continued without answering, because they both knew no other Peter was worth discussing, "but he's totally alone. And *then*"—she paused dramatically—"he sits across from Julia, like, in the same booth."

As Aimee paused to let the news sink in, Maggie's head swirled with explanations. "Maybe they were studying? Or working on a project? I heard the Spanish class has to do major presentations, so maybe they're both—"

"No books. They just sat and talked."

"Oh." Looking down and noticing her belly sticking out of her shorts, Maggie covered it with a nearby sweatshirt. "Do you know what they said?"

"No, but they seemed pretty serious."

Pretty serious? What could Peter possibly be discussing seriously with Julia Swanson?

"Anyway," Aimee continued when Maggie didn't immediately respond, "I know you have to go and I have to go pretend to read *Macbeth* in front of Mom, but I just wanted to give you the scoop."

"Okay," Maggie said, picking at small hole in the sweatshirt on her lap.

"Call me later?"

"Okay," Maggie said again. If Aimee had been reporting on someone else, someone she didn't fall asleep thinking about at night, this news would've prompted a barrage of questions. How long did they stay? Did they share a glazed donut? Did they lean toward each other while talking? Was there any touching above (hands) or below (feet) the table?

Did they seem *together*, or just hanging out? But because it was Peter, she could only think of one. "Aim? Do you think he likes her?"

"I don't know, Mags," Aimee said quietly. Then, more assured, "But I don't see how he could. She's really not very nice. So, no, there's no way. But if he does, it's totally time to move on."

Right. There was no way Peter could like Julia because she wasn't very nice. The truth was she wasn't very nice to *Maggie*. Maybe she was actually a saint who cared for her ailing grandmother and rescued cats from the animal shelter.

Probably not, but why else would Peter sit in her Krispy Kreme booth?

"Well, thanks for the scoop." She pushed the pillow to the floor, stood, and pulled the scale from underneath her bed. "Enjoy *Macbeth*. I'll call you later."

She'd weighed herself that morning, but had only eaten a garden salad and handful of pretzels since. Surely she'd burned those calories throughout the day, plus at least five hundred more doing Richard Simmons. Suddenly desperate for reassurance, she pulled the scale out from under the bed and tugged off her shorts. After making sure the needle was set exactly at zero, she stepped on gently and looked straight ahead while the dial jumped.

177. No change.

Throwing a T-shirt over her head before she could catch her reflection in the mirror above her dresser, she lay back on her bed and crossed her arms over her face. Maybe the whole thing really was just one big joke. Because who was she kidding? No matter how much weight she lost, she'd probably never be as thin as Julia or any other girl boys liked. And Water Wings tryouts were less than a week away, she'd *just* begun practicing at Mud Puddle Lake, and Richard Simmons wasn't going to make one bit of difference now, no matter how many leg lifts he cheered her through. It was too late. She'd dug herself into too deep a hole. Maybe Aimee could convince her again next year. Maybe 365 more days might be enough time.

And if that was the case, day 366 was far enough away that she could delay her transformation by ten more minutes.

Before her brain could talk sense into her body, Maggie hopped off the bed and dropped to her knees. What harm could one little piece do? And what difference would it really make, anyway? She was tired, her entire body ached, and even though the pounds were coming off, she'd never lose forty more pounds before tryouts, if ever.

Her heart pounded in nervous anticipation instead of

physical exertion, and she lowered her head till her chin touched the floor and she could peer through the darkness under the mattress. She reached with both hands and sifted through abandoned socks and crumpled notebook paper, longing for the familiar, reassuring sensation of candy foil against her skin. She shimmied on her knees up and down the length of her bed, but she'd been frustratingly thorough in her chocolate cleansing. She sat up and crossed her arms over her stomach. Had she been able to think of anything other than the task at hand, she might've noticed that her crossed arms lay slightly lower, because her stomach was slightly flatter.

She jumped up and dashed to her closet. She pulled pants off of hangers, rifled through their pockets. Dragged old purses down from the top shelf and turned them inside out. Sweaters, boxes, bags—anything with compartments, slots, or openings—she pulled apart and rummaged through until she stood knee-deep in a mountain of closet debris, her chest swelling and dropping and her heart drumming in her ears.

She sank to her knees and her eyes brimmed with tears.

Tears that might've overflowed onto her sticky cheeks, if not for a small piece of shiny silver across the room.

Her breath caught in her throat as she crawled out of the

pile and across the floor toward the nightstand. She thought she might cry as she grabbed the miniature Hershey bar, held it to her nose, and inhaled the sweet scent through the wrapper. It had been almost two weeks, a stretch longer than any she'd known in more than six months. She didn't know how she'd missed this one piece, but she'd never been so grateful for such an oversight.

Her fingers trembled as she tore open the foil and tossed it to the floor. The smooth chocolate grew slippery under her skin and she closed her eyes and brought it to her lips before it could melt completely.

"Sweetie, aren't you eating?" her mother called through the door.

Maggie's eyes snapped open and saw the clothes and bags littering her floor as though some random intruder had made the mess, and the blue screen of the forgotten television.

She shook her head, cleared her throat.

What had she almost done?

"Not hungry, Mom."

She waited until her mother's footsteps retreated back down the hallway before standing up, rewrapping the uneaten chocolate bar, and throwing it into the trash basket underneath her desk.

She took off her T-shirt, wiped her fingers on the damp cotton, and tossed it on the floor. She redid her ponytail and tightened her shoelaces.

Stood with her hands on her hips and breathed deeply. Waited thirty more seconds and pressed Play.

23.

"Okay, gum poppers!" Ms. Pinkerton bellowed into her megaphone. "As your runny mascara and frizzy hair have probably indicated, it's raining outside."

Maggie breathed a sigh of relief from her seated position in the top of the bleachers. Bad weather usually meant relaxing games of Horse around the indoor basketball hoops.

"Yes, Ms. Snodgrass?" Ms. Pinkerton bellowed.

Genevieve stopped waving her hand in the air, covered her ears, and winced.

"Ms. Pinkerton, I'm right in front of you."

"So?" the megaphone screeched once.

Genevieve rolled her eyes and kept her palms close to the sides of her head, in case of another sudden outburst. "What about our championship softball tournament?"

Maggie shook her head. Her first thought upon looking out the window that morning was that the scheduled game, the last of their entire softball unit, would be canceled.

"Rest assured, Ms. Snodgrass, the worst hurricane has yet to wash away these playing fields." She lowered the megaphone to her side, and raised it again. "Unfortunately."

"So we'll reschedule?"

"Yes, Ms. Snodgrass." Ms. Pinkerton cleared her throat before tilting the megaphone higher to better address the entire class. "Balls are in the closet, laps are around the perimeter of the room. Stay out of one another's and, more importantly, my way." She snapped off the megaphone, did an about-face, and ducked into her office.

"Glad to see the rain hasn't affected her mood," Aimee joked.

They stood up and began the slow descent down the bleachers. Following the majority of girls across the gymnasium floor to the equipment closet, they retrieved two basketballs and slowly dribbled their way to the sagging hoop.

"So, how's training?" Maggie asked, hoping her voice didn't betray her nervousness. She'd been so busy with her own training that they hadn't seen much of each other recently. And whenever they had talked, Maggie usually tried to steer conversation away from tryouts. But it hadn't been mentioned in so long, she feared Aimee would think she'd forgotten, or else was too preoccupied to care.

Aimee nodded and passed her basketball from one hand to the other. "Not bad. I feel like Flipper, but I think it's really paying off. My time's down, the routines are memorized. Now it's just a matter of remembering to smile!"

Maggie glanced around to make sure they were distanced enough from the rest of the group. "Just think of how good it'll feel to show Anabel and Julia. That'd leave me smiling for days."

Aimee looked up and frowned slightly. "Show them what?"

"That you're good enough." Maggie bounced the ball, focused on keeping her voice level. "That you can do anything they can do."

"I already know that." Aimee shrugged. "That's not why I'm trying out."

"Right, of course not." Maggie shook her head to dismiss such a silly thought. In her pursuit of proving something, she'd forgotten every other Water Wings hopeful tried out for the same reasons: to make friends, swim every day, and just have fun.

They stopped walking and stood to the right of the basketball hoop.

"So, how're things with you?" Aimee bounced her ball to Maggie as Maggie bounced hers back.

"Fine." Maggie dropped her basketball and then Aimee's as it returned. Aimee's voice was too casual. She obviously wanted to know much more than just how "things" were—like why Maggie had fallen off the planet, for starters.

But now was not the time for explanations, so Maggie scrambled after the balls instead of elaborating. She purposely tapped one with the toe of her sneaker, sending it skittering across the floor and buying more time.

"Do you mind?"

Maggie glanced up to see Julia standing in the middle of the court with one hand on her hip.

Maggie stopped one ball with her fingertips and dropped to her knees to grab the other before it rolled out of reach.

"We're sort of in the middle of a game." Julia raised her eyes to the sagging hoop, under which Maggie now crouched, and back to Maggie without moving a muscle.

"Sorry." She felt her face burn as she brought both balls to her chest and awkwardly regained her footing.

Aimee jogged over, took a ball from Maggie's arms, and walked with her off the court.

"So, how are classes?" Maggie continued their conversation as though nothing had happened. "Are your parents—"

Maggie's voice broke and the ball fell to the floor as something hard and swift knocked into her shoulder.

"Oops!" Julia giggled. "*So* sorry, Maggie! It slipped right outta my hands!"

As Aimee spun around to glare at Maggie's antagonist, Maggie rubbed her shoulder and hurried after the ball. It rolled without slowing down right toward Ms. Pinkerton's office, so she broke into a jog, leaned over, and reached as far as her arms would allow. The last thing she needed was an impromptu reprimand for not keeping the ball on the court. She imagined Ms. Pinkerton bursting through her office door, raising the megaphone, and announcing Maggie's latest klutzy performance loud enough for the entire school to hear. After which, with her luck, the year book photographer would show up to timelessly capture her ball chase and later add the caption *Maggie Bean: so close, yet so far.*

The ball didn't stop until it bounced up against Ms. Pinkerton's door, opened it slightly, and hopped into the office.

Maggie skidded to a stop just outside the office door and moved quickly against the wall to avoid being seen. She held her breath, her heart threatening to shatter from the sudden exertion, and waited for the orange ball to come hurtling through the doorway.

Out of the corner of her eye she saw Aimee talking to Julia and wished she could hear what was being said. Aimee could instill fear in anyone just by talking quietly and keeping a straight face. She was always so cheerful that on the rare occasion she wasn't, everyone knew something had to be very wrong. And even despite Maggie's recent disappearing act, Aimee still stood in her defense, arms crossed and shaking her head as Julia feverishly talked and gestured.

Her back flat against the wall, Maggie shuffled closer until she could peek into the office. Spotting a gray filing cabinet, she wondered if Ms. Pinkerton kept extensive notes on their performances. Her gym grade was always the lowest on her report card, though the consistent B was certainly better than what she felt she deserved. Fortunately every gym teacher she'd ever had had given major points for effort, but it was Ms. Pinkerton's first semester and report cards weren't due for another two months. Who knew what she could do to Maggie's GPA?

Noting that the bottom drawer of the filing cabinet stuck out, Maggie kept her back and palms against the wall and shuffled even closer, craning her neck when the contents of the drawer came into view. She tilted so far forward one foot raised off the ground.

There were no files, manuals, or extra megaphone

batteries. No first aid kits, whistles, or ice packs. Nothing that she suspected might come standard in any gym teacher's office. Inside the bottom drawer of Ms. Pinkerton's filing cabinet were five snack bags of Cheetos, two packs of Ring Dings, four envelopes of hot chocolate, one big bag of Twizzlers, and three packets of Otis Spunkmeyer cookies.

"Can I help you, Ms. Bean?"

Maggie barely heard Ms. Pinkerton but managed to quickly stand up straight in the doorway. As she did, she noticed the unoccupied megaphone handle sticking over the side of the desk.

"No, I was just, that is, the ball rolled—"

She stopped. She'd glanced up to meet Ms. Pinkerton's eyes, but had become instantly distracted by the white powder framing her lips and dotting her chin. She watched as Ms. Pinkerton quickly brushed a stack of crumbs off her desk and into the palm of her hand and shifted a pile of papers over the Hostess donut box. Her mouth fell open as Ms. Pinkerton's cheeks turned bright red and droplets of perspiration sprouted on her forehead.

"Bean," she said without looking up.

Maggie shook her head. "Right, sorry."

Leaving the ball, Maggie gently closed Ms. Pinkerton's office door and hurried across the gym.

24.

"Hey, what is this? Nap time?" Arnie playfully scolded.

Maggie opened her eyes and held one hand to her face to block the sun's glare.

"Don't you know tryouts are mere days away?"

"I thought you were watching Oprah give away brand new houses to her entire studio audience," she teased.

Arnie crouched beside her feet.

"Commercial break." He lowered himself farther till he was fully seated on the dock. "And by the way, Oprah's people *really* need to start thinking about their male viewing population. I'm a pretty sensitive guy, and even *I* get tired of learning about the latest and greatest in feminine products." He tossed a pebble into the water. "Which, by the way, doesn't seem to be much."

She laughed and sat up from her full body stretch. "Kind of like peanut butter on celery sticks. You really can't disguise it as anything better than it is."

"*Any*way!" he exclaimed, clapping his hands together. "Only a few days to go. Are the butterflies fluttering?"

She dangled her legs over the side of the dock as she thought about the state of her nerves. It was hard to tell if the recent, regular gnawing in her stomach was from butterflies or hunger.

"Not yet, I don't think. Practicing here has actually been surprisingly relaxing—like being on vacation, except for the whole arctic temperature thing."

"Do you have the routines memorized? Wanna do a run-through in front of your own live studio audience?" He sat up straight and folded his hands in his lap to demonstrate his attentiveness. "You don't even have to give me anything."

"I will if you will." She raised her eyebrows.

He turned his head slightly. "Intriguing." He resumed his slump forward and shoved his hands back into his sweatshirt pockets. "But I don't know any of the moves. Sorry."

"No!" She laughed. "I'll show you the routine *if* you play your flute for me." She suggested this without thinking twice. He didn't even like admitting that he owned such a "girly" instrument, so there was no way he'd voluntarily perform.

"Sitting through an entire hour of feminine product updates is more appealing than that."

"Fine," she said smugly.

"But!" He jumped up, brushed dried leaves off his pants. "If we're going to be future business partners, it's important that we each know who we're really dealing with, don't you think?"

Her mouth fell open as she watched him hurry down the dock, up the backyard, and across the deck to the house.

"Please tell me that's a portable lie detector test," she said when he returned with a small black box. Any other way of getting to know each other had to be better than her offer. She'd love to hear him play, but only if her applause was enough of an exchange.

He sat down next to her and gently placed the box on his lap. She hardly noticed, but Arnie was a big guy, and the case against his legs looked as small as the husband's briefcase in Summer's dollhouse.

"The commercial break's over, by the way. You see how important I find our future business."

She bit back the grin that teased her lips. She never thought of Arnie the way she thought about Peter Applewood, but she was still thrilled by his strictly platonic and potentially profit-driven interest.

"It's very pretty," she offered after he'd gingerly unfastened the silver clasps and opened the case.

He shot her a look. "This is a very serious instrument. Without it, the greatest musical masterpieces would never be heard. The fact that it's shiny, silver, and *pretty* is completely irrelevant."

She rolled her eyes. "So play already, maestro."

Arnie cleared his throat, raised the flute, and inhaled deeply.

Maggie's eyes widened. He hadn't been kidding. Five years of private lessons *had* taught him well, because the music that followed was clear, crisp, and flawless, even outside, where the greatest acoustics came from the pine tree branches overhead.

She watched his fingers for a few minutes before leaning back on her elbows and closing her eyes. She momentarily forgot her original reason for wanting to come to Mud Puddle Lake and thought instead of how she grew more relaxed with each afternoon spent with Arnie. If nothing else came from Pound Patrollers besides their introduction, not another pound lost or smaller size worn, she might still forgive her father for signing her up.

"So?"

Her eyes snapped open.

"No applause, pats on the back, roses at my feet?"

She looked up as he put the flute back in its case.

"I reached my grand finale two minutes ago and you're over there, sleeping."

She laughed. "That was really, really good." She sat up and playfully punched his shoulder. "You really *can* play the girly flute. I'm impressed!"

He shrugged and reddened slightly. His fingers fumbled with the silver clasps.

"Your turn!" he exclaimed in relief as he snapped the case shut.

She covered her face with both hands and shook her head.

"C'mon! I just busted out the thin lip for you!"

She crossed her arms over her chest and racked her brain for some way to get out of it. Headache, sort throat, sudden case of the sniffles. Or, better still, cramps, to complement his commercial viewing. But she knew he would never seriously make her, and he would never be seriously annoyed if she chose not to, even despite his own performance.

She uncovered her face. Looked at the lake, Arnie, and back at the lake. Inhaling deeply, she stood up, straightened her sweats, and wished it were somehow possible to swim fully clothed.

"You know you don't have to," he offered, his voice suddenly serious.

She met his eyes, which were more visible than usual underneath his red knit cap. She nodded, smiled slightly and wondered if he could see her heart pounding through her chest.

"Could you just—" She motioned to his head. "I mean, until I'm like—" She gestured to the water.

Without question or hesitation, he pulled on the red fabric of his hat until his eyes were completely covered and turned his head away from her.

She took three deep breaths before unzipping and removing her sweatshirt, tugging off her sweatpants, and facing the lake in her skirted bathing suit.

Facing the lake in her skirted bathing suit, two feet from a *boy*.

She closed her eyes, pretended Arnie was an abandoned inner tube, pictured the routine, and, before her brain could get the best of her, jumped.

25.

Maggie cut off Richard Simmons's farewell air kiss, muted the television, and patted her face, arms, and legs with a towel. She tugged off her damp shorts and sports bra, pulled on her bathrobe, and checked her appearance in the mirror to see if she could pass for having just finished a tough homework assignment and not forty-five minutes of cardio. Satisfied, she listened at her door to make sure the hallway was clear before throwing it open and dashing to the bathroom.

She locked the door behind her, turned on the shower, and leaned against the counter, chest heaving. She'd stretched for ten minutes after completing the workout, but her heart still raced as though she were running in place. She closed her eyes and forced deep breaths. Ever since she'd upped her exercise time to three hours a day, her stamina had lessened considerably and she'd felt weaker instead of stronger. She knew she was pushing it, but felt she had no choice. Time was running out, and she was desperate.

When her temples finally stopped throbbing, she slid the shower curtain open and shut without getting in so that no one questioned her bathroom activities, and dropped her robe to the floor.

She pulled the scale away from the wall, quickly checking to make sure the dial held steady at zero. With only two days left before Water Wings, there was no time for mechanical errors. The morning reading had been disappointing, down only one pound since the day before to 170. To make up for it, she'd had only an orange at lunch and a piece of chicken at dinner, and had done Richard Simmons twice. She expected much improvement in the evening weigh-in.

She kicked off her underwear, looked straight ahead, and gently stepped one foot, then the other onto the scale. She closed her eyes and willed whatever food particles remained in her body to fizzle into nothing. She crossed her fingers and toes, held her breath, opened one eye, and looked down.

171.

Her stomach jumped.

She backed off the scale, moved the dial up, down, and back to zero. She ripped the ponytail elastic out of her hair, removed her small silver earrings, and laid them on the counter. Took a deep breath and stepped back on.

171.

How was she possibly *up* a pound? Drastic measures brought drastic results, and she'd assumed after eating only 500 calories the entire day and exercising for an extra 45 minutes, she'd at *least* be down to 169.

Her stomach lurched again. She stepped off the scale and wrapped her robe around her shoulders.

As the steam from the shower filled the room, Maggie closed her eyes and lowered herself to the bathtub's edge. Her head swirled slowly as the throbbing returned to her temples. She'd vowed never to throw up as part of her weight loss efforts, but right then it was all she wanted to do. And not because she hadn't met that day's target, but because she thought it was the only thing that might make her head and stomach stop spinning. She leaned forward and rested her forehead on her knees.

She must've sat like that for a while because—

"Maggie, honey!"

She opened her eyes.

"Sweetie, are you okay? You've been in there a very long time." Her mother's voice was concerned as she knocked on the door.

"Fine." She cleared her throat. "I'm fine," she said louder, lifting her head. She'd been resting on the tub's edge so long she could barely see the bathroom door through the steam.

Willing her body to hang in there a just little while longer, she slid off her robe, climbed into the shower, and rested her palms on the wet tiles as the water poured over her.

Two more days. Just forty-eight short hours and it would all pay off.

26.

The day before tryouts, Maggie stood at the end of the dock on Mud Puddle Lake, her toes curling over its edge. It was her very last chance to practice, and she shook so much from the cold and nerves, the water below her rippled. She was thankful that Arnie had an afternoon band rehearsal so that she didn't have to talk about how nervous she really was, or endure well-meaning pep talks that would only worsen the shaking.

She looked straight ahead, avoiding her reflection without even thinking about it. Her stomach growled and she ignored the hollow feeling inside, the one she'd grown used to in the past week.

She held her nose and jumped into the chilled autumn water before her goosebumps convinced her to throw her sweats back on and go home. She ran through the routine three times, focusing more each time on the fluidity of her movements and pretending that she was already a graceful, confident team member. She practiced until the sky turned gold, then gray, and her stomach felt like it was starting to gnaw away at itself.

She hurried out of the water to her towel, shivering in the cold, sunless air. She was sure she resembled a Jell-O jiggler, she trembled so much, and was once again grateful to have the lake to herself.

She patted her arms and legs as quickly as she could, leaned over and squeezed the extra water out of her hair. As she lifted her head back up, it began to spin and her legs gave slightly. She closed her eyes and stood still, waiting for the dizziness to pass. Red, blue, and green flashed behind her eyelids, and she clutched her churning stomach with two hands, willing it to stop moving.

Before Maggie knew what was happening, before she could reach her hands in front of her to break her landing or lower herself to the ground, her knees shook once more before giving up, and she was only slightly aware that she was falling down.

When she awoke, Maggie was so warm and comfortable she snuggled deeper into her comforter without opening her eyes. She rolled over and was still for a few minutes, enjoying the peace and quiet and the faint smell of cinnamon. The house was silent. She couldn't even hear the dull murmur of the television through her door. The pain in her stomach reminded her that she was still hungry, so she instinctively and dazedly reached underneath her mattress, hoping her fingers would find Peanut M&M's first.

When she brought a fuzzy green sock to her mouth, her eyes popped open and she sat straight up.

She was lying on a brown suede couch under a plaid flannel blanket. A fire burned in the stone fireplace across from where she sat. She'd gone to sleep and awakened in an L.L. Bean catalog. In the mirror above the fireplace she saw the reflection of a window, and when she turned around to look through the actual glass, she saw the dark outline of Mud Puddle Lake.

What on earth was she doing in Arnie's living room?

She sprung from the couch and stood in the middle of the normally inviting room. There was firewood in a copper tray by the fireplace, a circular woven rug covering the worn hardwood floor, and fishing poles leaning against a coat rack by the front door. Everything was just as she'd come to know it, except for a brown corduroy jacket hanging from the coatrack.

She wasn't alone.

Maggie closed her eyes and rapidly shook her head back and forth. Not convinced she wasn't dreaming, she reached one hand to the top of her head and pulled a strand of hair out of her scalp. It hurt. She was definitely awake.

She quietly folded the flannel blanket and laid it on the back of the couch. She was now alert enough to remember swimming after school and the awful sensation that had overtaken her as she dried off, and could only guess that she'd fainted.

Being in Arnie's living room should've been comforting, except that it was dark outside, he'd had afternoon band rehearsal, and the corduroy jacket hanging on the coat rack was definitely too small for him, so her pulse quickened and her palms grew moist.

Because even if one of his parents or another relative had found her and dragged her to the house, the idea of anyone seeing her in such a state was just as terrifying as if she'd been kidnapped.

She tiptoed over to a chair that held her sweatpants, sweatshirt, and towel, and quickly dressed before heading toward the front door. She had no idea what time it was (it could've been weeks since she'd gone swimming, for all she knew) or what had really happened, but she didn't really want to know. As long as she made it out of the house, she'd make her jiggly legs move like lightning back home.

"You're awake, thank God!"

Maggie stopped, one sweaty palm on the doorknob. Her heart pounded so hard that she was sure the smooth-as-glass lake had white caps by now. But it pounded not because she feared who stood behind her, but because she would've known that voice in a crowd of a thousand tenors, all singing the same song.

Eyes closed, she turned slowly around, grateful for at least the small favor of time to put on her sweats.

"Hi, Peter."

27.

"So, cousins, huh?"

"Our mothers are sisters."

"Lovely."

Maggie didn't know which was worse: the fact that Arnie and Peter were related and that Peter might know about Pound Patrollers and anything else she'd opened her big mouth about, or that Peter was the one who'd found her and dragged her off the dock, up the yard, and into the house. She could only think about one or the other, because the combination was enough to send her diving back into the lake, forever.

He handed her a cup of hot tea as he came into the living room from the kitchen and sat on the floor near the fire.

"He didn't mention it because he thought you'd appreciate your privacy."

"And he was right."

She sipped the tea, momentarily distracted by how nice it felt to have something warm in her stomach.

"So." She squinted in anticipation of what he'd say next. "Was I, like, lying on the dock?" She pictured newspaper photos of beached sea creatures, defenseless and blubbery on a crowded shore of onlookers.

He tilted his head, and she silently begged him to stop trying to so accurately recall the scene.

"You were sort of half on, half off."

She raised her eyebrows.

"Your fingertips and hair were dangling fish bait in the water." He looked at her and smiled shyly.

She nodded and hid behind her hand. "I'm sure that was quite the sight."

"I was just relieved you weren't dead, to be honest."

"At least that would've saved me from a fate far worse: death by embarrassment."

He laughed. She smiled into her cup, in spite of herself.

"And how on earth did you get me up the hill and into your house?" Because beached sea creatures usually required lots of help, like dozens of strong arms to roll them across the sand and into the water, or the less time-consuming forklift.

"You came around for a bit and were able to make the walk to the house, but you were pretty out of it. Once I led you to the couch, you were out like a light."

"How'd you find me? Did you just happen to look out the window when you heard the loud crash? Did you think a house had collapsed or something?"

She couldn't believe she was pursuing this conversation, but his smile relaxed her, and she somehow knew that he smiled not because he found the situation funny, but because he really was relieved that she was okay. That made it easier to joke.

"I saw you practicing, actually."

Okay, easier, but not a piece of cake.

"Oh." Her voice was small. She quickly tried to recall any behavior potentially more embarrassing than her already blush-igniting aqua aerobics. She hoped her bathing suit had at least stayed put in all of the right places.

Peter turned his head, grabbed an iron poker with one hand, and sifted the fire's embers before turning back toward her. He seemed embarrassed.

"It was an accident, I promise. I mean, Arnie had mentioned you guys were hanging out here in the afternoons, but since he had rehearsal today, I figured the place would be empty."

"Do you come here a lot?"

He nodded. "Every day after school, since quitting the baseball team."

"You *quit*? But you're the reason anyone goes to the games!" She quickly looked into her mug. Just when she thought she couldn't *possibly* be more embarrassed.

"I just wasn't feeling it anymore and started coming here instead of having to explain to my parents why I wasn't at practice."

She nodded. "I can understand that."

"So, tryouts are tomorrow, right?" he asked, changing the subject.

She shrugged, pretending to discover a bothersome hangnail on her right pinkie. "Four o'clock, but it's no big deal."

"I don't know anyone else practicing that much."

"Aimee's in the pool every day."

"Okay, I don't know anyone else practicing that much in ice-cold lake water."

"It does seem to be a solo operation."

She waited for him to ask why she didn't just use the pool with Aimee.

"Well," he said, downing his cup before meeting her eyes, "I'm just happy you're okay. You are, right? Just recovering from a cold or something?"

Not eating in twenty-six hours seemed enough like an illness, so she nodded. "Yeah, thought it was a weird forty-eight-hour bug, but it might be stretching into the seventy-two-hour range."

They sat quietly but not uncomfortably. He turned his head slightly and she watched him watching the fire. As he stretched his legs in front of him and leaned back on his hands, the fire cast a warm light around his silhouette.

Her stomach turned suddenly. This feeling, she knew, wasn't hunger.

"Speaking of parents, I should probably call mine," she said, more brightly than she felt. Despite the potentially socially crippling events that had brought them together, she was sitting and having an actual, coherent, and occasionally even witty conversation with Peter Applewood, and she wasn't looking forward to leaving.

"Actually, it was getting late, so I called my folks and told them a bunch of the guys were going out for pizza, and then called yours to tell them you were coming."

Her mouth fell open. "How'd you get my phone number?"

"You're the only Bean in the white pages."

Maggie covered her face with her hands.

"What's wrong?"

"Nothing." She shook her head. "They just won't believe it."

"Believe what? That you'd go out for pizza?"

She laughed. "No, *that* they'd believe. It's the baseball team part they'd question."

"Do you not like baseball players?"

She felt herself turn red and restrained from fanning her face with her hand. Had those magazines taught her nothing? She was sure she shouldn't be this honest with someone she so wanted to impress.

"Maggie!"

Her head spun toward the front door as it flew open and slammed shut.

"Are you okay? I came as soon as I got Pete's message." He nodded to Peter before dashing to the couch and kneeling on the ground in front of her.

"I'm fine," she said sheepishly. "Just a little bug, it's nothing."

She brought the empty cup to her lips and tilted it up until her eyes were hidden. She felt him watching her and knew that if anyone could guess what had really caused her stunning episode, it was Arnie.

"Right, well." He stood up when she didn't say anything more, walked back to the door, and retrieved the three plastic bags he'd dropped.

"Steamed chicken, vegetables, and brown rice." He held the bags out to her.

Maggie lowered the cup, looked at the bags, and then met his eyes, which were almost sad underneath his red knit cap.

"You need to eat," he said quietly.

—

28.

"Oh my gosh, that bathing suit is just so cute! Where'd you find it?"

"J.Crew, but *yours* is adorable! The aqua really brings out your lemon juice highlights."

"You think? They're totally fading from the summer—"

"No way. They're fabulous!"

Maggie stood still in the cramped bathroom stall, drinking orange juice and waiting for a lull in the shrill locker room conversation. She looked down at her new red one piece, the one she'd bought on clearance over the weekend, when they'd taken an unexpected trip to the mall for new sneakers for Summer. It was a little small—a size fourteen when a sixteen would've done—but skimming past her old size eighteen had been so exciting, she couldn't stop.

"We are so gonna nail this," J.Crew said to Lemon Juice.

"Totally," Lemon Juice agreed. "These spots were made just for us."

"I heard it was a last-minute decision to add the two spots, and that Annie and Jules really fought for the extra girls."

Maggie swallowed loudly. Annie and Jules. Anabel and Julia. The cocaptains.

These two knew them on familiar terms. Not a good sign.

"Annie told me that too!"

They both gasped. Maggie pictured their perfectly manicured hands covering their perky chests. Were these really the sorts of girls with whom she was so determined to spend every weekday afternoon?

"Do you think she told us both because she had us specifically in mind?"

Maggie stood up straight and sucked in her stomach as the girls squealed in the locker room, down the hallway, and through the door leading to the pool. She waited in the stall, reading the pairings of initials scratched or penned on the door, trying to decipher the alphabetic love codes to distract herself a few minutes longer.

TA & MG. AL & UD. CC & RH. Togetha 4-eva.

MB & PA. She briefly considered scratching her own

perfect pairing on the door, right below the door handle so that no one would notice and wonder about the new addition.

She heard the last bare feet patter quickly down the hallway and through the pool door. Her watch said 4:05, which meant even the latecomers should've been out now, awaiting instructions. Maggie took one final breath and opened the door. Before throwing out the empty orange juice carton, she checked the nutritional information. Reminding herself that orange juice was *good* for her, she tried not to be alarmed by its 160 calories and whopping *thirty-two* grams of sugar.

"Maggie?"

"Anabel, hi." She quickly covered her stomach with her jeans and sweatshirt.

Anabel's eyes traveled up from Maggie's bare toes to her red face.

"So, tryouts, huh?" Maggie nodded as though standing half-naked while conversing with a Water Wing cocaptain was totally normal.

"Yeah," Anabel agreed, eyebrows furrowed. "Are you——?"

"Me? Trying out?" She shook her head. "Nope. No way." She looked down, crossed one leg over the other.

"So why are you——?"

"I was just on my way to the pool. At a gym. In another town."

"Huh." Anabel nodded. "They don't have locker rooms there?"

Maggie sighed. Her cheeks were on fire and her eyes refused to meet Anabel's. Lying was useless.

"I was *going* to try out," she admitted.

Anabel smiled slightly.

"But I changed my mind."

"Why?"

Maggie shrugged. "Something came up." There was no way she'd make it out there now. Anabel would tell Julia, who'd tell the other judges, and then she wouldn't stand a chance.

"Just now? In the bathroom stall?"

"Yup! So anyway, I might as well go to a gym in another town, now that I'm all dressed up."

"Right." Anabel nodded and bit her lip.

"But good luck out there. I'm sure your new team members will be great." She forced a smile.

"You could still try out, you know."

Maggie's mouth fell open. Anabel wasn't laughing. How was she not laughing?

"I mean, anyone can. And if you've been practicing"—she shrugged—"why not?"

Maggie forced her mouth closed as Anabel grabbed a granola bar from her locker, turned on one heel, and disappeared through the pool door. Was she imagining things? Had the orange juice sugar gone right to her brain? She padded over to the door and watched Anabel take her place behind the judges' table.

She hurried to her locker, shoved her clothes in her backpack, and grabbed the school pool towel, the one she was forced to use since misplacing her extra-large yellow striped towel. She wrapped the terry cloth as best she could, successfully covering herself from chest to mid-thigh, and headed for the door, ready for (just about) anything.

"Okay girls, here's the drill!" Ms. Pinkerton boomed into the megaphone.

Maggie crept quietly behind the bleachers, inches away from the backs of dozens of spectators. She ducked and lifted her head as the cranky gym teacher talked, peering between the bright wool sweaters and corduroy jackets, searching for the best spot to wait her turn, where she could see and not be seen. She'd added her name to the list that had been hanging up for two weeks just before she'd entered the locker room, and expected to watch most of the tryouts before her name was called.

"You're going to start in groups of five, one group at a time!"

Maggie froze, clutched her towel in tightened fingers. Groups? Holding her breath and peeking through a tan suede jacket and an orange wool sweater, she saw the other girls, about twenty in all, standing beside the pool, already gathered in small clusters. When had those been chosen? How did she miss that? She'd signed up late, but there had been no note about any registration deadline or anything at all about group assignments. Had there been all sorts of try-out rehearsals she'd missed out on too, because she'd been too busy numbing her butt and passing out at Mud Puddle Lake? Had she been paying so much attention to calories, fat, and carbohydrate grams that she'd grown completely oblivious to the things she actually needed to know in order to avoid looking like a complete idiot?

Heat sprung to her cheeks. She wiped the sudden perspiration with a corner of the towel. No one even knew she was there and she was already embarrassed.

"So!" Ms. Pinkerton boomed. "Do we have everyone?" She looked down at the black clipboard with the sign-up sheet Maggie'd just penned her name to. She was quiet for a moment, reading down the list, her finger still pressing the megaphone so that the names she mumbled under her breath sputtered across the natatorium in an unidentifiable garble.

Maggie waited, held her breath, braced for her unplanned revealing once her name was read. She waited, but nothing happened.

Was that even the right list? Had someone erased her name?

Ms. Pinkerton's head shot up. She scanned the excited girls at her side and the spectators on the bleachers in front of her. She looked back down at the clipboard, a puzzled look briefly altering her normally unwavering scowl and narrowed eyes, and then back up to the stands.

Ms. Pinkerton was apparently extremely confused, so much so that she actually lowered the megaphone.

"Is there no one else?"

If she hadn't been watching, Maggie would never have recognized the soft voice. It was almost melodic.

Ms. Pinkerton cleared her throat, tried to project. "*Everyone* who wants to try out is already standing next to me?"

Maggie looked up as the spectators shifted in their seats. If Ms. Pinkerton was referring to her, why didn't she just call out her name?

"If any of you have ever done it before, tried out for anything, faced any sort of competition, then you can guess how nerve-racking this may be."

The clusters of girls exchanged confused looks.

"And not every young woman is automatically pro-grammed with the confidence needed to get out in front of you, me, the judges, and their peers, and give it their all," Ms. Pinkerton continued, her normal voice loud enough to travel to the highest bleacher but uncharacteristically quiet enough to keep people from covering their ears in protest.

Maggie closed her eyes. How on earth was she supposed to come out from her hiding spot after *that*?

"But," Ms. Pinkerton continued, scanning the crowd again, "it takes a certain character to even get this far, and no matter what happens in this pool, these girls are to be con-gratulated. Let's remember that."

Maggie raised her eyes as the wool, corduroy, and denim shifted on the metal seats above her. The spectators looked at one another, probably wondering what brought on the unexpected introduction.

Maggie closed her towel more tightly around her chest, ready to take advantage of the stand shuffling, and make a quick, unnoticeable exit back to the locker room.

She bent down briefly to straighten the bottom of her towel and cover her thighs. She'd be happy to toss the stu-pid thing into the school hamper and never see it again. She stood back up and retucked the top folds so that there was no danger of her cover-up accidentally revealing more than she wanted as she dashed back to the locker room.

"Okay, then!"

Maggie's head snapped up as Ms. Pinkerton once again took to the megaphone.

And wished she'd wrapped the towel around her head instead.

The orange wool sweater and tan suede jacket, behind which she'd hid, had bent forward to talk to a green corduroy jacket and navy peacoat sitting on the bleacher in front of them. And looking right above them and at her, meeting her eyes with a slight, surprised smile, was Ms. Pinkerton.

29.

Ms. Pinkerton raised her eyebrows, just enough that only those who were really looking would notice, but remained silent.

Maggie bit her lip, the only body part not temporarily paralyzed. The cranky gym coach was actually giving her a choice. And there were a million reasons why it was such a bad, bad idea, but what came to mind instead were the reasons why it wasn't the *worst* idea. She'd worked for the motivation to even admit to wanting to try out, and then worked at physically preparing, and she didn't want even one reason discounting any of that now. She stood in a brand-new, skirtless red bathing suit, which she'd worked to wear, and which she deserved to wear. So without giving herself even one extra second to change her mind, Maggie nodded.

She moved without thinking and hurried to one end of

the bleachers. The farther along she moved, the stronger the scent of chlorine became, till it tickled her nostrils and she could taste it on her lips. And she smiled in relief, because unlike the bitter Mud Puddle Lake water, the chlorine still tasted as sweet as the chocolate she hadn't touched in over two weeks, the way it had when she'd swum with Aimee and hadn't thought about anything other than how good she felt.

She could do this.

"Maggie!" Aimee exclaimed as Maggie rounded the corner.

The rest of the girls turned toward her, nineteen mouths falling open in disbelief. Maggie focused on Aimee as she hurried across the slick tile, eager to finally reveal why she'd been lying low.

Aimee held her arms open and Maggie squeezed her tightly, feeling the tension that had built during the past few weeks melt away.

"I'm so sorry I didn't tell you!"

Aimee pulled away and held Maggie at arm's length, looking her up and down. The towel had slipped off after the embrace. "Mags, you look amazing!" she exclaimed, a wide smile illuminating her turquoise eyes.

"I'm so sorry, Aim. It was just something I needed to do on my own, you know?" Maggie said quickly and quietly.

The rest of the girls talked together behind cupped palms, the crowd discussed its own confusion in hushed voices on the bleachers, and Ms. Pinkerton busily cleared up the delay at the judges' table, but at that moment, no one needed an explanation more than Aimee.

"I knew something was up," Aimee whispered, "but I didn't really know *what* till I came out of the locker room a few minutes ago."

Maggie pulled slightly away.

"You have a fan club, my dear." Aimee nodded toward the bleachers.

Maggie turned her head slowly toward the stands. In the first row sat Maggie's mom and Summer, her mom's crossed legs bouncing in nervous excitement and Summer's small hands clutching two miniature pom-poms from last year's Halloween costume. When they saw that she saw them, their faces erupted in smiles wider than any she'd seen in months, and they waved furiously and flashed two thumbs up.

Maggie laughed and waved before turning back to Aimee. "Did you know I was doing this?"

Aimee's eyes widened. "Of course not! I just thought you were buried under extra-credit assignments."

Ms. Pinkerton called to the first group to enter the water.

"But then how did they know I'd be here?" Maggie hadn't even so much as spoken to anyone about her plans besides—

Aimee nodded her head back to the bleachers.

Maggie squinted and scanned the crowd again. She waved to Mr. and Mrs. McDougall. Saw Sherry Sherwood, a classmate who worked at the Ice Cream Shack. That was it. Those were most definitely the only people she knew. The only people she even recognized, besides—

Arnie and Peter Applewood. Maggie covered her open mouth with one hand. Arnie held a small blue cardboard sign with *Smile, BEANie Baby! This One's Yours!* in glittery block letters. She wasn't so over-the-top excited that she thought Peter was there for her and not Julia, but her heart still flipped when he smiled and waved.

Maggie laughed once, nervous, and waved timidly before turning away from the bleachers completely.

"Seems like you have *much* to tell me over dinner!" Aimee teased.

Before Maggie could answer, Ms. Pinkerton's voice boomed from the megaphone.

"Okay, girls, let's see some water wonder, shall we? Group one, you're up!"

The group of girls hopped into the water, stood by the

wall, and watched five Water Wings members gracefully perform the basic routine the group would reenact. Ten feet and fifty toes all met in the middle of one perfect circle as the Water Wings floated without drifting on their backs, and Ms. Pinkerton hurried over to Maggie and dropped the megaphone to her side.

"Group five, Bean," she instructed quickly before turning on one foot and storming away.

Maggie didn't know what to pay more attention to: the exchange of nervous glances by the members of group five standing just down the pool's edge, or the fact that Ms. Pinkerton had actually singled her out again.

Between that and her personal cheerleading squad, it was shaping up to be a very unexpected afternoon.

As distracting as her new fan club was, Maggie guessed only fifteen minutes remained before she had to get in the water. Aimee had moved down the pool's edge with her group, and Maggie stood alone.

She stood just behind her group and clung to her towel, shifting from one foot to the next and trying not to notice that while her bathing suit might have been a size fourteen and something for her to be personally proud of, her group members suits were definitely size fours or smaller. She tried to ignore the sharp edges of their shoulder blades, the narrowness of their calves, or the backs of their toned thighs, each of which was separated from the other by at least an inch.

Try as she had, her thighs were still very unfortunately affectionate with each other.

The first four groups finished quickly, and without a perfect performance. Angela Washburn had lost her footing, fell underwater, and came back up spouting water out of her nose. Ginny Vega had missed a cue and fallen so far behind, she'd pulled out of the circle entirely and pouted until the rest of her group had finished. Aimee had done a great job, but Missy Tooker accidentally swung one palm in the wrong direction and caught it upside Aimee's head, causing her to yelp in surprise.

As Maggie's group jumped into the water, she turned her head slightly to the stands. Peter, Arnie, her mother, and Summer all watched with wide, encouraging smiles. She took a deep breath and faced the pool. This was it. There was no turning back. She closed her eyes and pretended the tile beneath her feet was the worn wood of Arnie's dock. She opened her eyes, dropped her towel as easily as if she still wore sweats underneath, lowered herself to the pool's edge, and slid in. The water was like a hot bath in comparison to Mud Puddle Lake, but Maggie shook anyway.

The five Water Wings took their positions and performed another brief routine for Maggie's group. Once hidden in the pool, it was much easier for Maggie to concentrate on the task at hand, and she focused on the basic movements and felt her legs and arms practicing discreetly underwater.

She floated on her back. Feeling the feet of the other girls near her own, she pretended they were her mother's and sister's, and that they were at the beach and not in the school pool. The thought was calming as she waited for their musical cue to sound overhead.

When the music started, Maggie took a deep breath and pictured every movement the Water Wings had just demonstrated. She'd recognized everything from the competition tapes she'd borrowed from the athletic department, so there was nothing new to worry about. Her head was clear, her mind focused, and she didn't even have to work hard at pretending the bleachers were empty or that she was all alone in the freezing October lake water with only the small-brained fish for spectators.

She didn't even flinch when the blonde on her right accidentally rolled into her or when the redhead on her left stretched her legs instead of her arms into the air. She'd seen it on TV shows of physical competitions: Competitors will hang from metal bars over the ocean for a new car or $25,000, their confidence unshakable until the weakening of one person who falls and reminds everyone else of their own fatigue. But Maggie was unfazed.

This prize was hers.

As the music ended and the girls climbed out of the water, Maggie's face turned a shade of red much lighter than that of her bathing suit—so light, her cheeks were almost pink . . . pale, carnation pink, instead of fuchsia or maroon. For once her heart pounded in excitement and not paralyzing embarrassment.

She'd nailed every move.

She closed her eyes and inhaled deeply the sweet scent of chlorine. The warm, moist air wrapped around her body like a baby's first blanket, and she raised her face to the soft afternoon sunlight filtering down from above. For the first time in as long as she could remember, her body felt healthy and strong, as though it had really given all it had—as though it'd been capable all along and had been waiting only for her cue.

30.

"Daddy, you should've seen her!" Summer squealed, dashing toward the couch.

He cleared his throat. "Seen who?"

"Maggie!" Summer threw her arms overhead and twirled. "She was like a ballerina in the water!"

Their mother closed the door behind them, her face flushed. "Really, Robert, I don't think I've ever seen her look like that. She was so sure of herself!"

Maggie bit back the smile that had been glued to her face all afternoon, since tryouts and through steamed chicken and broccoli at Mr. Chi's House of Chow with her mother, Summer, and the McDougalls. She'd aced the group performance and had even gotten a standing ovation from a third of the crowd (everyone who'd been seated somewhere near her family, whose enthusiasm was unavoidably infectious) after her solo performance.

"Congratulations." He flashed Maggie a small smile before lifting the remote off his chest and aiming it at the television.

Maggie saw her mother frown slightly as she glanced at the flickering screen. She shifted her eyes back to him, waited.

"Don't you want to know what she was *doing* when she looked so sure of herself?" her mother prompted, forcing the smile back to her face.

He sighed, then raised the remote again and turned off the television.

"What were you doing when you looked so sure of yourself." It should've been a question, but his voice stayed flat.

Maggie had been excited to tell her father where she'd been and what she'd done. She'd hoped he might even notice and be proud that she'd lost weight. But when he couldn't even look up from the television, her heart sank to her stomach and squashed any leftover butterflies.

"I tried out," she blurted after her mother's elbow nudged her, "for the Water Wings. Mom's old team." She flashed her mother a quick smile.

"Congratulations," he said again, turning the television back on.

"Well, I didn't actually make the team yet, but I think I did okay and have a pretty good shot."

"She even got a standing ovation!" Summer exclaimed.

"Yes, she's being very modest. She had to swim twice, by herself and in a group, and the bleachers were packed! And let me tell you, those routines are way more complicated than they used to be."

"That's great, Mag Pie." He shifted slightly and Maggie thought he might sit up to better converse, but then he pulled the throw blanket from the back of the couch, covered his legs, and rested the remote back on his chest. "Really, really great."

On any other day, she might've retreated to her room, annoyed yet defeated, but it wasn't just any other day. Her mother had been right. She'd looked sure of herself because, for once, she'd actually *felt* that way.

She marched across the room, snapped off the television, and blocked the remote's target so he couldn't turn it back on. Her mother's and Summer's mouths fell open as she put her hands on her hips and faced her father.

"What are you doing?" he demanded.

"I tried out for the synchronized *swim* team—not the chess club or the debate team. A real *sports* team."

He exhaled, closed his eyes, and rubbed them with the

forefinger and thumb of one hand. "Maggie, now is not a good time for me."

"But it's a good time for *me*."

He opened his eyes, looked at her warily. "I've had a hard day. You don't understand."

She shrugged. "Try me." Her heart fluttered in her chest.

"Please get out of the way." He raised the television remote.

"Why is watching TV more important than talking to us?"

"Maggie!" Her mother gasped.

"What?" She was on a roll and didn't care if she got in trouble. "All I'm saying is that if Dad ever looked up from the TV, he might notice that Summer grew an inch in the past few months, that I've lost almost twenty pounds, or that you worry so much about money, you hide in my room when I'm not there."

Her father shot her mother a confused look as Maggie took a step backward upon realizing what she'd just said aloud.

"I mean," she continued before she could lose her nerve, "things haven't exactly been a barrel of laughs the past six months. And I just don't understand why you're not doing more about the situation, why you don't even seem to be *try-ing*. You wanted me to try for my own good, and I did! So what about you?"

"Maggie." Sternness had replaced the surprise in her mother's voice.

Her father rubbed his temples.

"I tried."

"What?" She shook her head, momentarily uncertain he'd actually spoken.

He squeezed his eyes shut once more as though bracing himself. Opened them and looked at her.

"I *did* try." He grunted as he slowly sat up. He clasped his hands loosely between his knees and met her mother's confused gaze. "That job? The potential employment opportunity I'd talked about?"

Her mother nodded.

"It was with your uncle. I did what you wanted me to do. I called him up. We had lunch, talked shop. I convinced him that I was serious about working for him and righting things for us."

Her mother crossed her arms, shifted her weight from one foot to the other.

"And he said that he was looking to train someone, because he was getting tired and predicted retirement was just around the corner. And he said if I really was that serious, that he'd consider giving me a chance. And if I really worked hard and proved myself, that maybe my future in his furniture business would be very, very bright."

"You mean—"

He nodded. "That when the time came, he'd hand it over. To me. For us."

"Well, but that's incredible," her mother marveled as a small smile played at the corner of her lips. "I don't understand why you couldn't tell us this before."

Her father leaned back, rested his head on the couch, and looked to the ceiling.

"It's not happening."

The smile disappeared from her mother's face.

"I called today because I hadn't heard anything in a while, and he said that he was very sorry, but that he talked it over with your cousin, who apparently agreed to take over the responsibility."

Her mother sighed. Summer sank into an arm chair, disappointment clouding her bright blue eyes. Maggie was disappointed too. She'd imagined weekly dinners at Nora's, bumping into Peter Applewood and his family so frequently that their two parties would eventually converge. She'd continue to lose weight until she was able to dress up like everyone else in the restaurant, and maybe one day she'd lose enough that she'd let herself taste the extra-fattening, extra-yummy tiramisu.

As her father resumed his reclining position on the couch and pulled the blanket up to his chin, Maggie bolted from the living room. She grabbed her laptop from her bedroom and raced back down the hall.

"Here."

Her father looked at the computer skeptically.

"Take it." She leaned forward and stretched her arms.

"Maggie, what is this—"

"It's what comes next." She lowered the laptop to the coffee table, turned it on, and pulled up the Master Multi-tasker. "There," she said proudly. "Those are the names and phone numbers of every construction, landscaping, and swimming pool company in the area." She bent down and clicked. "And those are ads for all the available outdoor jobs from four different newspapers, including requirements, contact information, and salaries."

Her father sat up and pulled the computer closer. As he scrolled through the listings, Maggie winked at Summer.

"When did you do this?"

"We started two weeks ago and have been adding to it since. We were holding on to it because of your other potential opportunity, but . . ." Her voice trailed off.

"We?"

"Me, Summer, and Aimee."

Maggie's heart pounded as he examined their compilation. She hadn't intended to present the information so abruptly, but if she hadn't done it then, he might've given up completely.

Her mother joined her father on the couch. "You girls were very thorough." She nodded approvingly as she read along.

"I know it's hard," Maggie continued. "But you can do it! I just wore a bathing suit in front of a hundred people. Two weeks ago I'd have hidden under the bleachers." She said this lightly, hoping to convince him that nothing was as bad as it seemed.

Her father closed the laptop and pushed it toward Maggie.

Her heart sank.

"Congratulations on the tryouts, Mag Pie." He lay back down and turned on the television.

She looked to Summer, then her mother. They were silent.

Leaving the laptop on the coffee table, Maggie headed slowly down the hallway.

Once inside her bedroom, she closed the door, flopped onto her bed, and felt her breathing slowly return to normal. She'd just said all the things she'd wanted to say for six whole months—all of the things she'd never *intended* to say, at least not to her father.

She knew Water Wings would change her life, but she couldn't have predicted this.

31. "Maggie, you were awesome yesterday!"

She felt her cheeks warm, smiled slightly, and tucked her hair behind one ear. Peter Applewood walked right next to her toward their lockers and she refused to freak out.

"Thanks."

"No, really. All that self-inflicted torture in the lake really paid off. You were just really, really good—better than pretty much everyone else who tried out."

She laughed. "Okay, what do I have that you want?"

They stopped in front of their lockers.

Peter looked at her, confused. "Huh?"

"I mean, I think I did *okay*, but I'm sure lots of girls did better. So you must want something!" Her hair fell out from behind her ear and covered the left side of her face as she spun her locker combination.

36 dates, 24 phone calls, 36 kisses.

"No, really!" he exclaimed. "I was hanging around the judges' table afterward——"

"Waiting for Julia," Maggie added without thinking. All sorts of things had been flying out of her mouth since try-outs.

"And I——what?" he asked when her comment registered. "Why would I be waiting for Julia?" He shook his head quickly and continued. "Anyway, I heard the judges talking and your name definitely came up more than once. They were really impressed. I think I even heard one of them say that you were a natural!"

Maggie looked at him, her heart still flipping from his reaction to her Julia assumption, and noted that he hadn't yet opened his locker. Had he not even needed to go to his locker and just wanted to walk with her? The books in her hands suddenly grew slippery.

"Really?" She quickly searched her vocabulary-saturated mind for words that *sounded* like "natural," but that meant something more along the lines of "disaster," "catastrophe," "nightmare." But her mind had somehow gone mushy and capable of focusing only on one thing.

Dozens of people milled around them, shouting, laughing, and running. On any day before today Maggie would've retrieved her books and rushed to her next class, head down, shoulders slumped, and focused only on her next forty-five-minute academic undertaking and not the faces or words of those around her. But today she was actually engaged in a normal, between-bell conversation, like anyone else.

A normal, between-bell conversation with Peter Applewood—which really was completely and totally abnormal, but which, Maggie hoped beyond hope, might slowly become a regular occurrence.

"Maybe my stellar performance had something to do with a certain sparkly sign?"

"Hey, you *earned* that sign."

"Well, you and Arnie are certainly gifted in the ways of construction paper and glue sticks."

"And glitter," he reminded her.

"And of *course*, glitter!"

"We took kindergarten very seriously." He cleared his throat and leaned against his closed locker. "So, the announcements are today, right?"

"They post the list after lunch." She wrinkled her nose in nervous anticipation.

"Well, I have no doubts you'll make it—"

"I don't—" She tried to cut him off, shook her head.

He held one finger to his lips, grinned, and started again. "I have no doubts you'll make it, and I'll be so psyched for you, but kind of disappointed, too."

Disappointed? Did he think she really wasn't Water Wing material? Was he afraid for her that she'd pass out again and make a fool of herself?

She shook her head again, waited for him to clarify.

He raised his eyebrows, waited for her to figure it out.

She didn't.

"If you make it, then you'll probably take your practicing to the pool, right? With the rest of the team?"

"I guess it'd be the thing to do, yes."

"So if you take to practicing in the pool, then that means you won't need the lake anymore?"

"I think the eight o'clock winter sunrise, four forty-five winter sunset, and eventual freezing over of the water might play small roles in the transition too."

"True. But whatever the reason, it means that Arnie and I will have to spend many an afternoon in that big house all by ourselves."

She tried to contain the sudden bubbles of delight that filled her belly and threatened to cascade out of her mouth in laughter.

"Just don't forget about us little people, that's all I ask."

She couldn't speak, so she nodded and smiled and hoped her face didn't reveal the dance party her heart and stomach threw inside her body.

The bell rang, and Maggie looked up to the ceiling, shocked. She'd never not been seated comfortably in the classroom, textbook open and pen in hand, when the bell rang.

"Well, good luck. I can't wait to hear how it goes!" Peter called over his shoulder as he began jogging down the hallway.

Maggie waved quickly before getting the rest of her books and slamming her locker shut. As she hurried through the emptying halls, her heart raced at what might be in store for the new Maggie Bean.

She couldn't believe her arrival had taken so long.

"Oh God, Aim. I don't think I can look," Maggie whispered at the back of the gathered crowd. They'd raced over to the locker room right after lunch but still seemed to be the last arrivals, the rest of the girls having staked out the place like Pound Patroller's Samuel had for the grand opening of the new Krispy Kreme.

"I don't want to look either, but just remember we've got as good a chance as anyone else here."

Maggie nodded and watched as twenty other girls bobbed, whispered, and eyed one another suspiciously. Maggie checked her watch. The announcement was late. Why was it late? Were there doubts? Had she made it yesterday and now someone was suddenly changing her mind in the logical light of a new day? But too much had happened. This meant far too much for her not to have made it.

And she couldn't think about what life would be like if her name wasn't on the list. She pictured it, *Maggie Bean*, right above *Aimee McDougall*.

The group of girls suddenly erupted in hushed whispers. Maggie and Aimee watched as Ms. Pinkerton came through the pool door with Anabel and Julia close behind.

Maggie reached down for Aimee's hand, clutched it in her own.

"Since you all seem to be here," Ms. Pinkerton shouted, silencing the group, "if you can shut your mouths for two seconds I'll go ahead and read the names of the new team members, to save you all from death by stampede and me from death by annoyance."

Aimee squeezed Maggie's fingers.

"Oh, and in case you care, I'm going to read three names instead of two, because the judges just couldn't narrow it down any more than that."

Maggie raised her eyebrows quickly at Aimee. The sympathetic, supportive Ms. Pinkerton of yesterday had apparently withered back into the regular old crank pot overnight.

"You two got anything to add?" She glared at Anabel and Julia.

Julia snapped a green gum bubble and shook her head while Anabel silently looked at the floor.

"Okay!" She sighed and looked down at the list.

Maggie thought she saw Ms. Pinkerton frown slightly and shake her head.

"Isabella Parker!"

Maggie watched J.Crew jump up and down, clap, squeal, and squeeze anyone who'd let her, not seeming to mind that she was still the competition.

"Next victim!" Ms. Pinkerton shouted.

Maggie squeezed Aimee's hand.

Two names to go. They still had a shot.

"Aimee McDougall!"

Maggie's heart sprung. Aimee's mouth, initially wide in disbelief, slowly turned up, and she covered it with two hands, her turquoise eyes crinkling in the corners. Maggie raised her arms in excitement, and they bounced up and down in a sloppy embrace. Aimee's grades had improved enough over the past few weeks that her parents agreed to let her join the team if she made it. Now she had, and deserved it more than anyone.

"This next one is yours, Mags! It has to be!" Aimee whispered gleefully, squeezing both of Maggie's hands.

They turned back toward Ms. Pinkerton. Maggie thought her heart might shatter into a million little pieces if Ms. Pinkerton didn't hurry and read the last name.

She closed her eyes, then opened them again when Ms. Pinkerton remained silent, frowned, and shook her head again.

"Last victim!"

Maggie bit her lip and tried to ignore the loud silence that had fallen across the group. She thought of the silver bathing suit, the weight she'd continue to lose, the practices, meets, parties. This one moment had the ability to change *everything* Maggie hated about herself.

"Jillian Zimmerman!"

And there it was.

Her heart pounded once more in protest before shattering into a million pieces and floating defenselessly through her body.

Double the squeals from the right meant that Lemon Juice had made the team with J.Crew. The rest of the girls burst into moans, groans, and other assorted declarations of disappointment as they turned toward one another in consolation.

Ms. Pinkerton handed the clipboard off to Anabel with one swift motion to her abdomen and walked back through the pool door in a huff.

Maggie stood without moving. She couldn't look at Aimee, who circled around to embrace her, or at Julia, who snapped her stupid minty gum at the front of the group as though she just didn't care, as though this decision had meant absolutely *nothing* to her, or at Anabel, who hid behind the clipboard. And she most certainly couldn't look at herself, her hands, legs, feet, the body that just wasn't good enough to get her what she'd so desperately longed for.

She hadn't done it. She'd worked so hard, tried everything she could think of to make herself look and perform better, and it just hadn't been enough. It wasn't her. She was never meant to be one of them. She didn't know how on earth she'd let herself believe otherwise for even a second. Why she'd let herself even entertain the *idea* that maybe she might actually have a chance to be something other than the socially crippled, overweight bookworm.

Because just like that, it was over. Done. The new Maggie Bean had disappeared.

Just *who* did she think she was, anyway?

32.

"Maggie!" Her dad called through her bedroom door for the fourth time in ten minutes. "You have five minutes!"

Maggie covered her head with a pillow and rolled over to the wall, as far away from the door as possible. She'd been napping for three hours, since getting home from school. If her dad would only stop making so much noise, she could very easily sleep through the rest of the night, the next day, and every day after that.

Because two weeks after Water Wings tryouts, energy was in short supply. She'd had way more when she wasn't eating anything, and now she was eating all the time, whenever, whatever she could get her hands on, and was more exhausted than she ever remembered being. Too tired to get out of bed in the morning, she was either late to school or completely absent. She was too tired to do her school-work anyway, so skipping didn't seem like a big deal. On the days she actually made it, seeing Julia waiting for Peter at his locker made her too tired to stay after for any of her clubs, so she came home, watched soaps, napped, watched more television, and eventually went to sleep for the night. And she was too tired to make any kind of conversation, so she avoided Aimee during the day and her phone calls afterward, carried every single book with her whenever she made it to school to avoid Peter at her locker, and told her mother to tell Arnie she'd call him back, though she never would. Her grades were slipping, her friends and teachers were worried about her, and her mother thought something more terrible than not making the Water Wings had sunk Maggie into this state of nothingness, but none of it mattered. She was just too tired to care.

"I hope you're listening," her father continued. "I know I've been easy on you because of tryouts, but it's time to get focused!"

She waited until his footsteps retreated to the living room before removing the pillow from her head and roll-ing on her back. She stared at the ceiling, reached one hand to the ground, and lifted up the first bag her fingers grazed. Whoppers. Not her favorite, but she shoved a handful into her mouth anyway. Her dad would probably knock again in thirty seconds, so she was just biding her time.

Because she'd go to Pound Patrollers. It didn't matter. She planned to sit in the back of the room, avoid Arnie, and eat the steady supply of Reese's Pieces she'd already poured into her purse. Eating, it seemed, was the only thing she wasn't too tired for, so it had quickly become her favorite activity.

Although "favorite" was too strong a word. That implied that she enjoyed eating, which she didn't. She just did it to do something, because she was too tired to care to do anything else. She knew she'd probably gained back whatever weight she'd lost before tryouts, and that didn't matter either. It hadn't made a difference then, so why bother?

She heard her mother's gentle knock on the bedroom door.

"Maggie, honey. Aunt Violetta's here," she called softly, apologetically.

Maggie sighed, willed her legs over the edge of the bed, and lifted her torso up with a grunt. Had she not done it herself, she never would've believed that this body was the same one that had gone swimming for fourteen consecutive days. It just didn't seem to want to move.

She stood up with effort, reached for her purse, and

dropped the remaining chocolate-covered malt balls into the pool of Reese's Pieces. She'd already removed her wallet for more room, so she slipped a five-dollar bill into the candy, in case her aunt felt like stopping at Ben & Jerry's on the way home.

As she felt around the floor for her sneakers, her bare foot bumped into something cool and hard. She bent one knee and dragged the scale out from under her bed.

How bad could it be?

Dropping her purse to the bed, she stepped onto the scale and closed her eyes. When the black dial had had enough time to settle in one place, she looked down.

183.

Only three pounds from where she started.

Without stepping from the scale, she pushed a mountain of clothes off of her laptop and loaded the Master Multi-tasker for the first time in two weeks. She clicked on "Water Wings" and scrolled down the list of weights to the very last one. She'd entered it on the morning of tryouts.

168. With a smiley face.

Sighing, she closed the laptop, backed off the scale, and pushed it under the bed. She found her sneakers, dug her feet into them without untying the laces, and let the weight of her heels press down so that her toes were all the way inside but the rest of her feet stuck out. She shuffled into the hallway, ignoring her parents' concerned looks as she headed out the door toward the car.

"Mag Pie, sugar lamb, what on earth happened to you?" Aunt Violetta exclaimed, looking Maggie up and down as she neared her on the front walk. Her aunt never got out of the car to meet Maggie—a single horn honking and headlight flashing usually sufficed—but apparently she'd been moving so slowly tonight, Aunt Violetta had been coming to check on her progress.

"Nothing," she answered dully, keeping her slow, steady pace down the front walk.

"Well 'scuse me for saying so, but that sure don't look like *nothing*." Aunt Violetta quickly covered the remaining distance between them and put her hands on Maggie's shoulders. "Your sweatshirt's on backward, your pants are inside out, your feet are hanging out of your shoes, your hair's standing up and out every which way like an electrocuted bird's nest, and your pretty eyes are sagging, sugar, *sagging*, like an old basset hound."

"Thanks."

"You trying to be funny, missy? Because I'm not laughing. I don't know what on earth is going on with you, but I tell you what—I'll figure it out by the end of the night, you can count on that."

Maggie looked at the ground, her purse growing heavy in the hand hanging at her side. Aunt Violetta dropped her hands from Maggie's shoulders and sighed.

"Well, come on. We've got a meeting to get to and no way am I going to let your sorry state make us late."

At another time, Maggie might've been insulted by Aunt Violetta's sidewalk scrutiny, but she knew she was right. She was a mess. The only difference was that her aunt seemed to care, while Maggie simply couldn't care less.

33.

Maggie let Aunt Violetta grab her by the hand and drag her into the meeting, and didn't resist until they headed right toward the circle of metal folding chairs around the pink scale. She wasn't about to join the happy circle, so she dug her feet into the ground and wouldn't move, like a leashed dog whose owner was trying to take him to the vet.

Aunt Violetta dropped Maggie's hand and spun around. "You are sitting next to me tonight."

"No, I'm not."

"Yes, you are. Because this isn't about being shy anymore, Maggie. This is about what's good for you."

What's good for you. Those words again. What *was* good for her? She thought she'd known, but it hadn't worked. She'd thought she'd had a chance, but it didn't matter. She'd done what was expected, she'd done what she thought people wanted her to do, and it hadn't made one bit of difference. How in the world would these people know any better? She'd heard Electra's words of wisdom: Get a goal, eat in moderation, exercise, reward yourself, and the benefits will follow. You'll be stronger, confident, outgoing, *happy*. She'd done all these things—had hardly eaten and spent hours exercising every single day—and had ended up with nothing. She knew she hadn't taken the healthiest approach (as proven by her stellar Mud Puddle Lake performance), but it was supposed to be temporary.

But Maggie had learned that it didn't matter what you did; it would never be enough in the eyes of those who'd already decided your fate.

"Aunt Violetta, don't bother. It's a waste of time."

Her aunt put her hands on her hips. "That's an awfully dumb comment from such a smart girl."

Other loud, happy Pound Patrollers streamed in. Maggie raised the hood of her sweatshirt over her head, crossed her arms over her chest, and flopped down in a metal folding chair by the snack table.

From inside her hood she watched her aunt's polka-dot shoe tap on the floor.

"Maggie." The shoe stopped tapping.

"Aunt Violetta." She slumped farther in the chair.

"Fine. Stay here. Nobody can help you but *you*." The polka-dot shoes spun around and hurried across the linoleum.

She heard without really listening as the rest of the Pound Patrollers took their places around the circle. She didn't pay attention to what they said, but she recognized the usual voices: Samuel, Electra, the gray-haired lady, the forty-year-old twins who wore the same outfits but in different colors. The only thing she *did* halfheartedly listen for was Arnie's voice, which she hadn't yet heard. But she'd managed to feign illness enough to skip last week's meeting, so he could've stopped coming or transferred locations, for all she knew. The thought was so disappointing she lifted her purse to her lap, unzipped it, and reached in until her fingers dipped into the reassuring pool of Reese's Pieces.

"Water stick?"

A piece of celery came at her from under her hood and her heart fluttered for the first time in weeks.

"No, thanks." She pulled back slightly, zipped her purse, and dropped it next to her chair.

The celery came an inch closer, offered her one last chance, and disappeared.

"Water stick with peanut butter?"

The celery reemerged.

She shook her head. Felt the beginning of a smile tickle her lips. Almost peeked out when her hood remained empty.

"Water stick with chocolate chip cookie dough?"

She laughed in spite of herself. Four celery sticks stuck out of a pint of ice cream whose construction paper label advertised *Arnie & Maggie's Very First Flavor*.

"Not bad, huh?" His face replaced the celery stick.

"Why's my name second? Who made that executive decision?"

"Mr. Al Phabet, m'dear. It's about the only perk associated with my name."

She slid the hood off her head and he leaned back in the chair next to hers.

"That's quite a supply you have." She nodded to the duffel bag at his feet.

He lifted out white bed sheets, waffle cones, and a head of broccoli.

"I didn't know how much selling you'd need."

She laughed. "I guess I should've held out."

While he shoved everything back into the bag and placed the ice cream on the snack table, Maggie sat up straighter, redid her ponytail, and shoved her feet all the way into her shoes. It was the most effort she'd put into her appearance in fourteen days.

"So," he said, patting his knees and facing her, "I'd hoped you'd be here."

She looked down, felt her cheeks redden. "Yeah, I'm sorry about—"

"Shh!" He closed his eyes and covered his ears with both hands, then opened one eye, then the other, and slowly lowered his hands once convinced she was quiet. "Don't apologize. You did nothing wrong."

She bit her lip to keep from protesting.

"I'm just glad to see you." He shoved his hands in his sweatshirt pocket. "You've been missed. Many people have been worried. Mud Puddle Lake has threatened to freeze over."

She sighed. "I'm totally fine. I've just been hiding out. It's silly, I know."

He shrugged. "I couldn't name one person who *doesn't* want to hide every now and then—except for maybe Samuel." He looked toward the circle where the most vocal Pound Patroller talked to a transfixed audience. "He's a bit of a social butterfly."

She laughed.

"Okay, but here's the deal. I know you're going through a thing right now—"

"It's not a—"

"And that's completely and totally understandable and I could launch into a whole big argument about those idiots at your school, but that's common knowledge by now, and the important thing is that I need a favor."

She raised her eyebrows. "Okay?"

He took a deep breath and bounced his knees up and down. "Okay." He exhaled. "So our school band concert is in two weeks and every year after the concert is a small party at my parents' country club and it's *always* miserable, but my parents *always* make me go, and the only way I could possibly even imagine getting through another one is if there was some sort of entertainment."

She tilted her head and waited for more. "And?"

"And, so, not like you'd have to sing and dance or anything, but maybe if you just came with me? And we hung out?"

She watched his earlobes turn red.

"I don't know, Arnie." She sighed and looked down at her sweats, the same ones she'd trained in, the same ones she'd worn nonstop for three days in a row. "I'm not exactly a fashion maven these days."

"We'll wear togas. I don't care. Bad publicity is still publicity."

She tried to imagine herself getting dressed up to go anywhere. The last time she'd come close was when her family had gone to dinner at Nora's. She wouldn't even know where to begin. And even if she managed to find something to wear that still fit, she'd then have to inevitably converse with strangers, and she hadn't felt much like chatting with anyone in recent weeks, besides Arnie.

"You don't even have to sit through the concert if you don't want." He said this softer, as though he didn't really expect that she'd want to go to the concert—just like he didn't expect his parents to go.

She looked up and saw that he looked down as he waited for her answer. How could she say no? Especially when he seemed to need her support in the same way she'd relied on his only weeks before?

"Will you play a solo and dedicate it to me?" she asked before she could change her mind.

His head snapped up.

"And provide vocal accompaniment?"

He grabbed a celery stick from the ice cream melting on the snack table and held it in one fist. "I'll start right now, if you want."

She paused, scratched her chin, and pretended to think about it. "It would be for the long-term good of our business, of course."

"Of course." He grinned.

She met his eyes and smiled. Wardrobe concerns and social shyness would have to wait.

"Arnie, I wouldn't miss it."

34. "You're here!" Aimee dropped the sneakers she'd just pulled from her gym locker.

Maggie shrugged out of her backpack. "I figured kickboxing was one unit I could really get something out of." She unzipped the backpack and sifted through notebooks and papers.

"Are you okay? Have you been getting my messages?" Now that Maggie stood in front of her, evidence that she was indeed alive, Aimee's initial excitement quickly faded.

Maggie knew her unexplained disappearance would require major damage control. Having to start somewhere, she triumphantly pulled a small box from her backpack and held it out to Aimee with a nervous smile.

"What's this?"

"It's to go with my belated congratulations and apology."

"Mags, I would've been happy with a phone call."

"I know." She took a deep breath. "And I'm *so* sorry for disappearing. I sunk into a funk after tryouts, but that's no excuse for not talking to you. I'll call you three times a day from here on out to make up for it."

"Well, thanks, but I totally—"

"And," Maggie continued with what she thought was the most important part of her apology, "congratulations on making the team. No one deserved it more, and I'm very happy for you."

"There's *so* much you don't know about that," Aimee said, lowering her voice as Anabel's and Julia's unmistakable giggles floated over from the next aisle. "But first, I've been *dying* to tell you about Peter and Julia. She was totally stalking him! He never liked her, and when I saw them at Krispy Kreme he was trying to tell her as nicely as possible so she didn't totally freak like stalkers are known to—"

"Bean."

Maggie turned around to see Ms. Pinkerton standing at the end of their aisle.

"My office. Now." She spun on one heel and disappeared.

"Just open it really quick," she encouraged Aimee, patting the present in her lap. While she was pleased to hear the truth about Peter and Julia, the news barely registered in her excitement of hearing Aimee sound like Aimee. At this point the possibility of their friendship returning to normal was more important than keeping Ms. Pinkerton at bay.

As Aimee sat on the bench and unwrapped the present, Maggie went through her mental checklist of things to do. Her conversation with Arnie had motivated her to slowly crawl out of the bottomless bag of candy in which she'd hidden, and she'd arrived at school that morning prepared to talk to her teachers, get all of her missed assignments, explain things to Aimee, and say hello to Peter Applewood at their lockers. If her destiny was to be an overweight bookworm, then so be it. At least she'd be an overweight bookworm with good grades and friends.

"Maggie, these are great." Aimee held up the glittery purple swimming cap and matching goggles. "But that's one of the things we have to talk about. I don't know if I can use them."

"Why not?" Maggie asked, her face falling. "Is it your parents? Your grades? Because I'll go to your house right now and tell them I'm *so* officially your academic advisor—"

"Bean!" the megaphone blasted down the aisle.

"We'll talk later," Aimee assured with a small smile.

Maggie hugged her quickly before following Ms. Pinkerton.

"Sit."

Maggie sat in Ms. Pinkerton's office and peeked to her right to see if the filing cabinet of treats was open. It wasn't. A quick glance at the desk between them showed that it had been cleaned since Maggie's last visit.

"It's nice of you to join us."

Maggie nodded. "Sorry, I had some things to take care of."

"Would these things involve the results of the Water Wings tryouts?"

"Yup." There was no reason to deny it. A few weeks ago she would've stumbled over her words and worried about the best thing to say to keep Ms. Pinkerton happy, but not anymore.

"Have you talked to Ms. McDougall recently?"

Maggie met Ms. Pinkerton's gaze. "Actually, not really. Why?"

"Because she approached me the day after the results were announced, claiming that she wanted to decline her acceptance."

Maggie's mouth dropped open. "But that's crazy. She worked so hard. Why—"

"She overheard the Water Wings cocaptains discussing the results, and apparently Ms. Zimmerman's shouldn't have been the third name called."

Maggie nodded, waiting for more.

"*Yours* should've been."

Maggie's mouth fell open again.

"Now," Ms. Pinkerton brusquely continued, "teenage gossip interests me about as much as skinny dipping in February, but I decided to investigate, because there's nothing I hate more than the rich getting richer while the poor get poorer."

Maggie squinted. "Huh?"

"Ms. Bean." Ms. Pinkerton leaned across her desk and lowered her voice. "Everyone had the potential to receive three votes. One from the girls' regular swim coach, one from the guys' swim coach, and one combined from the team cocaptains."

Maggie's stomach turned. Just thinking about tryouts made her nerves tremble.

"You were awarded two out of three of those votes."

Maggie's eyes widened.

"And the cocaptains went to extreme measures, mostly involving temper tantrums and parental involvement, to sway the others." Ms. Pinkerton paused. "In a fair and just world, Bean, you'd be a Water Wing."

Maggie flopped against the back of her chair.

"Here's the deal." Ms. Pinkerton leaned back and crossed her arms over her chest. "I've taken it up with the powers that be and you have two options—well, three, if you don't find either of the first two appealing."

Maggie shook her head to try to clear it. None of this had been on her list of things to make right that day.

"One, you can join Water Wings."

Her heart raced in her chest and she crossed her arms over her stomach, which she now regretted letting grow since tryouts.

"Two, you can join the regular swim team."

She brought one hand to her forehead. Was this really happening?

"Three, you can give the entire athletic department the well-deserved finger and go about your business."

Maggie laughed and then quickly covered her mouth. She'd never seen anyone laugh in front of Ms. Pinkerton before.

"Personally, I'd be tempted by the third." She shrugged and looked at Maggie. "But I understand what this must mean to you. And I strongly recommend considering one of the other two."

"Wow." Maggie looked down and then back at Ms. Pinkerton. "Did Aimee definitely decline her acceptance?"

Ms. Pinkerton shook her head. "I encouraged her to stick with it, at least for now."

Maggie nodded.

"Bean, there's always going to be that person, or those *people*, who insist on making life difficult. But you can't let them stop you." She leaned across the desk toward Maggie. "You just can't."

35. Maggie stood in front of her closet, hands on her hips. She'd put it off for days, but it was time to make a decision. No amount of well-intentioned support would matter if she showed up to Arnie's concert in the blue bath towel currently tucked around her torso.

And it didn't help that her closet was a disaster area worthy of yards of yellow caution tape. After wrecking her room in search of that forgotten piece of chocolate, she'd shoved her old purses, pants, and sweaters back into any available nooks and crannies and leaned all her weight against the closet door to shut it. She'd basically lived in the same pair of sweats since then and hadn't surveyed the damage.

She sifted through the surviving blouses, skirts, and dresses and dismissed one after the next for being too bright, too dark, too old, too new, and, most frequently, too small.

She'd thrown out her most recent candy stash after meeting with Ms. Pinkerton and had been careful about what she'd eaten since then, but still feared the consequences of her posttraumatic binge. Sighing, she pulled out a gray wool skirt and white sweater and laid them across her bed.

She stepped back to inspect. Definitely boring, but her mother had bought the outfit for her at one of her highest weights, so any appeal was enhanced by its fitting potential.

"Maggie!"

She grabbed her robe. "Yes?"

Her father opened the door and stepped one foot inside before realizing her half-naked state, ducking back out, and shutting the door behind him.

"Oops! Sorry about that! Just let me know when you're done!"

She tied the robe around her waist, opened the door, and flopped on the bed.

"Hi." He stood in the doorway and crossed and uncrossed his arms. He leaned to one side, then the other.

"What's wrong?" She watched his nervousness.

"Wrong?" He shrugged, then shoved his hands in his pockets, took them out, and lowered them to his sides. "Nothing."

She raised her eyebrows.

"Is that what you're wearing tonight?" He took one step and leaned over to look at the outfit displayed behind her.

"Maybe."

"It's nice. You look nice in those colors."

She turned her head to make sure the skirt and sweater were still gray and white, and then looked at him, puzzled.

"So"—he clapped his hands together—"your mother told me about the swim team. That's great."

"Dad, do you want to tell me something?" She'd decided the day after her conversation with Ms. Pinkerton to accept the second option of joining the regular swim team instead of Water Wings. She agreed the news was great, but it was also two weeks old and no reason for him to be nervous.

He nodded, took a batch of rolled-up papers from his back pocket, and handed them to her.

"What's this?"

"Open it. Section C."

Maggie unfolded the papers, wrinkly and worn from much use.

Her father sat gently on the bed next to her.

"See"—he pointed as he spoke—"the black circles are jobs I've applied to. The red checks are those I've heard from. The green exclamation points are those I will interview for or have interviewed for." He squinted and pointed again. "And that brown dot is either coffee or mustard."

"Are these—"

"From your spreadsheet, yes. I printed them out and have been adding on."

"Wow." She was impressed.

"And this"—he reached into the pocket of his shirt and pulled out a sheet of gold stars—"is for when I get offered a job." He pulled out two more sheets. "Or jobs." He smiled.

She nodded. The papers were so marked up she could hardly read them, but it was easy to see almost as many green exclamation points as black circles.

"Dad, this is great." She nodded and smiled at him. "Really."

He shrugged. "I just wanted to show you. Hopefully we'll get some good news soon."

She rolled up the papers and handed them back.

"I think we already did."

He looked down and fiddled with the papers as though there was something more he wanted to say. He stood up, tucked the chair back underneath her desk, and headed toward the door.

She stood up and reached for her skirt and sweater.

"Maggie," he added, turning back around. "I was just in a rut, you know? They're hard to get out of sometimes."

She nodded thoughtfully. "I know." Because she did.

"I mean it. I know things haven't been easy. I know *I* haven't been easy."

She held the skirt and sweater to her chest. She didn't know what to say.

"I don't know what to say."

He looked up, surprised. "Nothing." He shook his head. "You don't have to say anything." He took one step toward her, leaned forward, and patted her arm. "I just want you to know we'll be okay."

She looked down at the skirt and sweater she still clutched, then walked toward him without raising her eyes. When she felt his arms awkwardly wrap around her, she dropped her clothes and squeezed him tightly, without worrying for even a second that she might crush him. She hadn't hugged someone like that in months.

After he'd left the room, Maggie checked her watch. She hadn't budgeted in a surprise guest appearance and didn't have time for mental replays, because she was now down to thirty-five minutes.

She took one last look at the outfit, untied her robe, and let it fall to her feet.

She closed her eyes, inhaled deeply and held her breath, just in case the skirt needed extra room to maneuver as she pulled it on. She put one leg through, then the other, grabbed the waistband with both hands and yanked up.

And almost fell on the bed.

She'd tugged as hard as she could so that the skirt could make it over her middle, but it had flown right up. She dropped the waistband. The skirt fell to her hips. Before the magical power disappeared, she threw on the sweater, turned to look in the mirror, and laughed. The white wool drooped around her.

She dashed to her closet and reached her arms as far back as they'd go. She pulled out the black velvet pants and blue cashmere sweater with the tags still on them that she'd received as Christmas gifts the year before. They hadn't fit then or since, but she'd kept them in the back of her closet, just in case.

Her heart pounding, she pulled the sweater over her head. She smiled to herself when it brushed against but didn't cling to her skin. She dropped to the bed, prepared to lie on her back and break her fingernails to get the pants on. She slid in one leg, then the other, her heart racing as the material slid up her calves. She stood up slightly to shimmy the pants over her thighs. They resisted only slightly before moving up and over her stomach and Maggie's mouth dropped as her fingers pushed the silver button in place without any fancy acrobatics.

She looked down at her stomach. It wasn't exactly flat, but it was definitely the closest thing to it she'd come in months. And her pink toenails were visible without her torso having to form a ninety-degree angle with her legs.

She had to look completely ridiculous. The outfit couldn't really fit *and* look halfway decent. She debated leaving the house without checking, in hopes that what she didn't know really couldn't hurt her. But deciding it could still hurt Arnie, she crossed the room and stood in front of the mirror.

She took a deep breath, closed her eyes, and thought of the swim team, Arnie, Aimee, Peter Applewood, and her father's job pursuit—every good thing she could imagine. She tried to convince herself that it didn't really matter what she saw when she opened her eyes.

And when she finally did open them, she almost fell on the bed again.

Because for the first time in as long as she could remember, Maggie looked in the mirror and liked what she saw.

36.

"I've gotta say, this is the best boring country club party I've ever been to." Arnie raised a champagne glass in the air.

"I don't know what you were whining about. This is my *first* boring country club party, and I already can't wait for the next!" Maggie leaned over to clink his glass with hers.

"More Diet Sprite?" Peter asked, coming into the living room with a new bottle.

"Your parents really won't worry when they realize you're not there?" Aimee asked, flopping on the couch next to Maggie.

"They won't realize, trust me." Arnie held up one hand in oath. "Coming here was a brilliant idea."

"Well," Peter said, raising his glass, "here's to a band concert unlike any before, and to a flute solo that rocked the house."

"Was that what that was?"

"Did the stars in your eyes cloud the standing ovation?" Maggie teased. "Which, by the way, I was very prepared to initiate had the rest of the audience not beat me to it."

Arnie winked at her from his seat near the fire.

"And here, also, to the best pitcher ever to return to the game," Arnie said proudly, raising his glass toward Peter.

Maggie's mouth fell open. "You're back on the team?"

Peter shrugged, his face turning red. "I missed it. My parents aside, I realized I hated not being out on the field."

"I know many girls who'll be happy to hear that!" Aimee said.

"And to Madame DuMonde's pop quiz queen *and* the newest Water Wing!" Maggie quickly interjected, before Aimee could say anything else that made Maggie blush even more. "Both very deserved accomplishments." She smiled and tapped Aimee's glass with her own.

"May you bring order and normalcy to the team," Peter added.

Maggie sipped her drink, Peter's words ringing in her ears. There were many reasons to be annoyed at the Water Wings, and reminders were everywhere. Even the couch she and Aimee now shared was the same one she'd awakened on after passing out by Mud Puddle Lake.

"And, of course," Arnie said, getting up from his seat near the fire to join them on the couch, "to Maggie. The best butterfly any water has ever known."

"And a solid party planner, too," Peter added, grabbing one of the dozens of balloons bobbing against the ceiling. "Thanks for inviting us along." He handed the balloon to Maggie and squeezed next to Arnie on the couch.

"There *are*, like, five other places to sit in here," Arnie commented, elbowing Maggie on one side and Peter on the other after they'd all toasted and sipped from their glasses.

"It's warmer this way," Aimee said, resting her head on Maggie's shoulder.

"Very cozy," Maggie agreed.

"Yeah, as warm and cozy as a *sauna* in *August*." Arnie fanned his face.

"Go jump in the lake," Peter suggested.

Arnie laughed and shook his head. "You're crazy. It's October."

"The water's like ice," Maggie explained.

Peter shrugged. "We know where to get warm."

"I'm in."

Maggie looked at Aimee. "You're *what?*"

"Why not? It'll be something fun to commemorate all of our accomplishments."

"That's what the bubbly and nice words are for," Arnie reminded her, raising his glass and shaking it slightly.

"I'm in too." Maggie stood up and held her hand out to Aimee.

"This *is* Diet Sprite, right?" Arnie sniffed his glass.

Aimee beamed as she took Maggie's hand and jumped up from the couch.

If the past few weeks had taught her anything, it was that nothing had to be out of character. Even jumping in a freezing lake, at night, fully-clothed, could be a completely *Maggie* thing to do if she wanted it to be.

"You really don't want to be the only one not doing it, do you?" Peter teased, standing next to Maggie.

"Peer pressure. From my own cousin." Arnie shook his head.

Maggie knelt in front of him. "Think of the business."

He raised his eyebrows. "Arnie and Maggie's ice cream?"

She nodded. "Employee morale."

"No fair." He pouted. "You know I can't refuse the good of the business."

She grinned and patted his knee. "I'll get the towels."

As Aimee and Peter ran outside, Maggie found the linen closet and pulled out four bath towels. Just as she was about to close the door, she noticed a triangle of yellow striped terry cloth peeking out from the top shelf. Her heart racing slightly, she pulled it down.

Her old beach towel, the same one she'd hidden under after Anabel and Julia had spotted her walking across the pool deck in her skirted bathing suit—the same one she'd wished she could've been hiding under when Peter found her sprawled across Arnie's dock. She must've left it there. She brought it to her nose and inhaled the clean scent.

"Oh, Magsie," Arnie called, "it'll soon be summer, the lake warmer, and employee morale shot if we don't hurry it up!"

Water Wings reminders were everywhere. And there really were a hundred reasons why they should bother her.

But as she shoved the beach towel back onto the top shelf and dashed down the hallway toward her friends and Mud Puddle Lake, she couldn't think of one.